and
pet
who

-new
cross
!

KAREN McCOMBIE

SCHOLASTIC

483110

For my big brother Fred, who taught me to read (not).
Love, KaKa x

Scholastic Children's Books
An imprint of Scholastic Ltd
Euston House, 24 Eversholt Street
London, NW1 1DB, UK
Registered office: Westfield Road, Southam, Warwickshire, CV47 0RA
SCHOLASTIC and associated logos are trademarks and or registered
trademarks of Scholastic Inc.

First published in the UK by Scholastic Children's Books, 2008

Text copyright © Karen McCombie, 2008
The right of Karen McCombie to be identified as the author of this work has
been asserted by her.

Cover illustration copyright © Rian Hughes, 2008

10 digit ISBN 1 407 10501 9
13 digit ISBN 978 1407 10501 7

Typeset by M Rules
Printed by CPI Bookmarque, Croydon, Surrey
Papers used by Scholastic Children's Books are made
from wood grown in sustainable forests.

3 5 7 9 10 8 6 4 2

This is a work of fiction. Names, characters, places, incidents and dialogues are
products of the author's imagination or are used fictitiously. Any resemblance
to actual people, living or dead, events or locales is entirely coincidental.

www.scholastic.co.uk/zone

Contents

Uh-oh, I'm doomed

I was in a bit of a grumpy mood.

I'd been in a grumpy mood for quite a while; about three years, actually.

I guess I got in a grumpy mood when my parents split up. I don't really mind about that now, but I think I just got into the habit of being grumpy. I guess I'm just not very good at happiness, and all that stuff.

Unlike Sonny. . .

"What's up with you?" Letitia asked, stopping chattering now that she'd somehow detected grumpiness at my end of the phone.

The cause of my current grumpiness? The racket coming from the rest of the house: Mum's classical music clashing with Will's frantic hoovering colliding with Martha's wailing overlapped by Gran's lullabying muddled with the bellowing of Sonny's loud-mouth best mate,

Kennedy. How was a girl meant to listen to her nice and chilled-out Magic Numbers CD?

Now *there's* something I'm never grumpy about: music. Listening to it, I mean – not playing it for real. I didn't inherit any of Mum's natural musician-y genes (unlike Sonny); I just inherited half of Dad's old rock music collection (don't tell Dad – he might come and ask for it back).

And the great thing is, music can give you a total buzz, but you don't have to appreciate it by going round grinning like a dork the whole time. (Hmm . . . now, who goes around grinning like a dork the whole time? Let me think. Ah, yes, *Sonny!*)

"*Nothing's* up with me," I lied to Letitia, as I gently placed flouro Post-It notes on Dog's rising and falling furry tummy. Dog is my cat. My cat's name, I mean. Yes, it is confusing. Yes, it was my idea (when I was five) to name our cat Dog. Sonny wanted to call her Mittens, because of her white paws, but I was in a bad mood because Sonny was in rehearsals to be a Cute Little Boy in our local North London drama club's production of something lame and was getting ninety per cent of Mum and Dad's attention (what's new?), so they sort of gave in and let me name our cat Dog to make up for it.

Hey, that's made me think: maybe I'd been grumpy for longer than I'd realized. . .

Letitia sighed. She didn't sound convinced by my obvious lie, but her need to bend someone's ear about her current Fantasy Boyfriend meant she was willing to throw caution to the wind and carry on, whether I was grumpy or not – or even *lying* or not. "I mean, he *is* cute, isn't he? Don't you think, Sadie?"

She'd already bored me about Stefan Yates during our lunch hour, so it was a pity she felt the need to bore me about him a bit more now, 'cause she was actually pretty all right as a friend when she wasn't drivelling on about useless crushes.

"I guess. . ." I mumbled, wondering how many Post-Its I could use up on Dog before she started flicking her fluffy tail in annoyance. Probably loads, 'cause Dog is very patient. She's had to put up with eight years of me doing non-cruel, but faintly stupid things to her in my many moments of boredom. She's never once hissed or scratched, even when I once tried to turn her into a robot by wrapping her in tinfoil.

Poor Dog. Maybe she should be less pleasant and slightly meaner, like Clyde. There's no way Clyde would patiently let people stick Post-It notes to his fur. He'd eat the first one, then wee

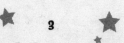

on your favourite shoes as a lesson, just to show you he's a rabbit who won't stand for any nonsense.

"And he's not just cute – he's kind of *deep* too. Don't you think?"

Letitia had absolutely no way of knowing whether Stefan Yates was "deep" or not. All she really knew for certain was that he was called Stefan Yates, he was three years above us at school, and he was in the Year Twelve tennis team, 'cause it said so in last week's school newsletter. But when Letitia gets a crush, she doesn't let small irritations like facts get in the way. She really seems to enjoy giving her Fantasy Boyfriends traits she's casually made up and then convinced herself to be true.

Well, a girl's got to have a hobby. Letty's other hobbies are gymnastics (she's very bendy) and giggling a lot (pretty infectious, and useful for getting me out of grumpy moods). Pity I wasn't watching her doing that backwards crab thing she can do so well, or giggling at something stupid with her right now. Pity her hobby of the moment was turning my brain to mush.

I leaned over towards my computer, aiming to quietly switch it on – muffling the *bing*! of the start-up – and email my other friend, Hannah,

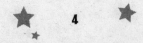

just to give my mushy brain a break. But a-*ha*!, it didn't take a detective to see that there'd been an intruder on my computer earlier. Not only was it switched on already, but as soon as the screen burst from black, there was the Arsenal Football Club website, featuring a huge photo of the flashy Emirates Stadium.

Sonny. Of course.

Who was meant to ASK first if he could use my computer while his was getting fixed, but who hadn't bothered. Of course.

What else had he been looking at? I checked the recent history. . . *The Stage* website for the entertainment industry. Of course.

The *Jackass* site, full of clips of stupid stunts. Of course.

Football mad, fame obsessed and easily amused by anything moronic: yep, that summed up my brother pretty neatly.

". . .so I *kind* of thought he was looking at me but then maybe the sun was just in his eyes. . ." Letitia prattled on.

Ah, Letitia, Letitia, Letitia. Did I mention that one of her other hobbies is reading the problem pages of magazines? Especially anything to do with relationships? It was a shame that Letitia never applied any of the advice to herself and lads. I tried it once, giving Letty the blunt "It's never going to happen" line about one of her Fantasy Boyfriends. She immediately looked like a watery-eyed, tiny bunny who'd just been kicked very hard and I felt like a complete louse, so I never bothered trying *that* again.

Still, since I didn't have ears with knobs to turn the volume down on, I clicked off the web browser instead and hit the messaging icon on my computer.

What's up? I keyed in, hoping Hannah was sitting by her computer, bursting with interesting news to tell me this Friday teatime. Maybe a rogue typhoon had just passed her house (Number 50) and was swirling destructively down the street towards our place (Number 135), swallowing cars, litter and little old ladies in its wake.

Nothing much, Hannah keyed back straight away. *Doing homework.*

So no typhoons imminent in our corner of London, then. The trees in Highbury Fields park weren't about to be blown down. Tables and chairs weren't about to be sucked up in a whirlwind, and torn from the front of the zillions of cafés and bars up and down nearby, bustling Islington. How dull.

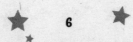

What're you up to? she keyed in some more.

Nothing much. Going to have a shower in a minute.

I was actually sitting in my knickers and bra (non-matching, I mean *badly* non-matching), as I'd been about to throw on my dressing gown and head to the bathroom to shower away a week's worth of school when Letitia had phoned.

Not that I was about to tell Hannah about Letitia's one-tracked, less-than-interesting conversation (still currently droning on in my left ear). I might like Hannah and Letty lots, but they're not too wild about each other. If I make even the weeniest, *slightly* negative comment about one to the other, they'll jump on it and make out it's a big thing, if you see what I mean. It's like they're in constant competition with each other to be The Best of my best friends. (Hey, guys – I'm *seriously* not worth it. . .)

At least it makes life – and friendship – easier that Hannah and I live on the same street, but she doesn't go to the same school as me and Letitia. (By the way, me and Letty: we've been mates since our first day at secondary school, when we were put next to each other in French class, and both ended up sniggering at the teacher's put-on French accent. As for Hannah: her family moved in to our road last year, and as soon as I spotted her making strangling motions behind her brother I knew we'd get along just great.)

Fancy going shopping tomorrow morning? Hannah emailed.

No, I didn't.

Hannah's shopping addiction is as boring as Letty's Fantasy Boyfriend fixation. The shops in Islington – on Upper Street, Essex Road and in the N1 shopping centre at the Angel – are all pretty amazing. There're high street shops, retro boutiques and scarily expensive designer-y places, where my messily-scuffed trainers suddenly stand out like they're luminous, or made of mud. But being made to reluctantly trudge round every single one of these places *twice* (once is never enough for Hannah to make her shopping choices) makes my head melt with the sheer tediousness of it all.

And here's a thing that sometimes worries me: do you suppose that being easily bored is the sign of a feeble brain?

If it is, then uh-oh, I'm doomed. . .

Can't – doing something else, I lied to Hannah, via email.

"It's not like *impossible* that he would notice me, is it, Sadie?" said Letitia. "I mean, if I get into

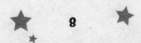

the tennis club at school, then who knows what could happen?"

You know, I could've sworn the volume of the rest of the house had just gone up. Will's manic hoovering definitely seemed louder (Mum's boyfriend likes to claim that he's very "New Man" and is happy to do more than his share of housework, but really I think he's covering up a bad case of Obsessive Compulsive Disorder). And everything else had gone up a decibel or twelve to compete.

"You're not really listening, are you, Sadie?"

"Yes, I am!" I lied to Letty.

"Well, I can hear you tapping. You're checking emails or something, aren't you?"

"I'm not! Honestly!" I protested, snatching my hands back from the keyboard as if the QWERTY alphabet was suddenly red-hot to the touch. "I'm stroking Dog, actually!"

Dog purred as soon as my hand ruffled her head, instantly forgiving me for the twenty-five fluoro Post-Its that had turned her into a day-glo patchwork cat.

"Hmmm," grumbled Letty, huffing. But not huffing for long. "Hey, fancy hanging out tomorrow morning?"

"Of course!"

I hoped I sounded enthusiastic. To be honest, I was worried that I'd just end up hearing about the talents and wondrousness of Stefan Yates face-to-face all over again (when it would be very difficult to hide my yawns of non-interest), but I felt so guilty that Letty had caught me out that I'd have said yes to her suggesting that we high-kick our way round the N1 centre, treating Saturday shoppers to choruses out of *High School Musical*. (Please, *please* don't let her want to do that. . .)

"OK. Speak to you in the morning, Sadie, and we can decide what to do then."

"Yeah, in the morning. See you."

And with no more Letty, and no more emails from Hannah for the moment (maybe she'd got side-tracked by some completely *fascinating* piece of homework), I stuck one last Post-It on Dog and stretched across my bed to turn up the volume on my CD.

"Sadie. . .?" came a voice from outside my bedroom door.

Peace, perfect peace. Wish I could have some of it round our house.

"Yeah, Sonny?"

Sadie and Sonny.

Sadie + Sonny.

My brother and I have known each other since we were a near-matching pair of microscopic eggs, nestled together. Actually, we might *not* have been nestled together: our mum's womb was probably Olympic stadium-sized to two organisms smaller than a pin-head. Maybe we were as far apart as two football fans at opposite sides of the Emirates Stadium, with Sonny doing pin-head-sized star jumps down *his* end and me at *my* end leaning my pin-head-sized ear up against the womb wall, trying to hear the music going on in the outside world.

But, naturally, it didn't *stay* that way. As our cells multiplied and divided, and multiplied and divided *who* knows how many more times, we both grew from bean-sized to actual baby-sized, and couldn't help but get close up, squashed and personal.

Sadie + Sonny = twins.

"What a blessing! They'll have a bond for life. . ." my gran had sighed when she'd gazed at our tiny-ness, as we shared a plastic cot next to Mum's hospital bed.

And what a bond twins have. Gran's got thirteen years' worth of cuttings about the psychic connections between twins. Her favourites are tales of twins separated at birth, who go on to do

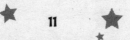

the same job, marry people with the same name, have matching illnesses and get on like a house on fire when they're accidentally reunited on their seventy-fifth birthdays or whatever.

As for me and Sonny, our own special bond is really something. Oops, sorry – I meant to say *nothing*. Our special bond is, like, non-existent.

"I'm telling you, the 'pull' will come when you're older," Gran once said sagely, when I disappointed her by informing her that I hadn't a clue what was going on in my brother's head at any given time. "When you're apart from each other, and there's some kind of crisis – *that's* when you'll tune in to each other."

Wise words there from Gran. Next thing, she'd be trying to convince me that the Tooth Fairy was absolutely genuine and that her number was in the phone book.

"The twins? Oh, they're so similar it's spooky!" she'd have probably loved to boast to her friends and neighbours. Instead, Sonny is so upbeat and annoyingly perky, perky, *perky* that spending an hour in his company leaves you feeling like you've been forcibly made to swim in lemonade and then rolled in icing sugar.

And me? Spending an hour in my company would be OK, I hope. Pretty normal, I guess. If you don't mind a bit of sarcasm, grumpiness and a few strange, boredom-busting habits. (Remind me: *why* do my friends fight over me?!)

"Hey, can I borrow that first Arctic Monkeys CD, Sadie, 'cause I was just telling Kennedy about that track – oh!"

We're supposed to have this small but important rule in our house: if a bedroom door is closed, you never, I mean NEVER, walk straight in. You knock first, then WAIT till you're invited. This small but important rule has been in place for about five years now, but Sonny STILL hasn't grasped it.

"You're not wearing anything!" Sonny stated, with an annoying grin on his stupid face, as he stood in the doorway of my room. (In that long, frozen moment of shock, I still – stupidly – managed to notice Clyde the rabbit hopping through the open door, happily chewing on some delicious, nutritious loo-roll that was unravelling its way behind him down the hall, and presumably ending in an empty cardboard roll on the holder by the toilet.)

"GET LOST, SONNY!" I yelled, suddenly coming to my senses and grabbing the first thing I could to try to cover myself up with it. Pity it was only what was left of the fluoro Post-It note pad. "AND I AM **NOT** NOT WEARING ANYTHING – I AM WEARING A **BRA** AND *PANTS*!!"

From somewhere halfway down the stairs, above the racket of hoovering and wailing etc., I heard Kennedy breaking into grunts of laughter. Fantastic.

"Sorry, Sadie!!" Sonny grinned sheepishly, hands shoved in the pockets of his baggy combat trousers. I noticed he wasn't moving, like he still thought he had a chance to get my Arctic Monkeys CD off me.

Yeah, *right*.

"I *SAID* GET **LOST**, SONNY!"

Tradition's a wonderful thing. And right on cue, Sonny did his traditional telltale yell to Mum, the same traditional telltale yell he's been doing since we were too little to remember. Nowadays, of course, he did it less to tell tales on me and more to plain wind me up. Which it did. Completely.

"MUM!" Stomp, stomp, stomp went Sonny down the stairs, as I leapt up and slammed the door shut. "Sadie said I had to get lost!!"

Sadie said this . . . Sadie said *that*. Sadie said this . . . Sadie said *that*.

I wish I could stop getting bugged by him

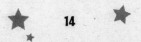

trotting out that same old line, 'cause it might stop him doing it in the first place.

"Oh, dear. Oh, well – never mind!" Mum would be dreamily answering him, as usual. I just couldn't hear 'cause of the slammed-shut door, the manic hoovering and a bunch of violins reaching a screechy crescendo.

Grr. I'd suddenly had enough of the madhouse that was home. I switched off my CD player and I grabbed my jeans – OK, eased them out gently from underneath Dog – and got myself dressed in three seconds flat (it's amazing the adrenalin rush you get from pure bra-and-pant embarrassment).

So long house, so long family.

It was high time I had a hot date with a Christmas tree. . .

The asylum-seeking Christmas tree

Dead people make very good neighbours.

They don't hoover outside your bedroom door, play classical music too loudly, or invite obnoxious friends called Kennedy around to visit.

On the flip-side, hopefully our noisy family doesn't disturb the endless sleep of the dead people who happen to be our neighbours. Well, *one* set of our neighbours. I mean, we've got regular *live* neighbours on either side of us; it just so happens that our garden backs on to a graveyard.

Letitia gets pretty creeped out by the graveyard, and doesn't like to hang out by the Christmas tree with me. She doesn't get that graveyards are actually pretty nice.

No – honestly, they are. They're peaceful and beautiful and quiet, and full of grass and flowers and tweeting birds and fluttery butterflies . . . all that sort of corny but nice stuff.

Actually, this is one of my favourite places to be. When the mood takes me (usually a *bad* mood, i.e. when Sonny's bugging me), I escape from the house, wriggle through the gap in the railing at the end of our garden and settle myself in my own private mini-wood. It's just an overgrown leafy corner, really, that the cemetery gardeners don't bother with.

Just as well – if they looked hard enough, they'd see there was a Christmas tree seeking asylum in amongst the hawthorn trees and holly bushes.

OK, let me tell you the tale of the Christmas tree. I'll try and keep my sarcasm levels to a minimum (difficult for me) since it's actually a *cute* sort of story. (By the way, I don't really like the words "cute" and "nice", but nobody's come up with a non-corny, much cooler option yet. Maybe *I* should try to, next time I'm bored. . .)

Ahem.

Anyway, back before Sonny and me ever existed, back when Mum and Dad were just Nicola and Max – i.e. when they were childless and carefree – they didn't bother with trees or decorations at Christmas; they celebrated by partying a lot.

They didn't even bother with a Christmas tree the first Christmas me and Sonny were around,

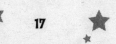

17

mainly because they were in a state of exhausted shock (goodbye partying, hello two sets of lungs doing synchronized screaming at three in the morning).

But Mum and Dad had sort of settled into family life by the time we got to be two years old (maybe because we screamed less and smiled more), and so Dad got all festive and came home one December day with a small fir tree in a bright red pot. Mum had been expecting a much bigger affair, and had cleared out a corner of the living room for it. Dad said he could see the disappointment in her face when he walked in, mainly because she'd already had fun spending way too much money on fairylights and fancy decorations that now wouldn't fit on such a diddy, little tree.

However, Dad figured the diddy tree was the exact same height as me and Sonny, and we'd be able to get involved and decorate it. And so Mum got down on her knees and helped us, untangling me and Sonny from strings of fairylights and stopping us from accidentally breaking delicate baubles and deliberately pinging branches into each other's faces.

Sonny says he can remember all of this. Yeah, *right*. He might be a genius at acting and singing

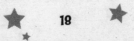

and dancing and all that stuff they teach him at stage school, but he's not an all-round genius with a photographic memory from toddler-hood or anything. (I blame the acting; I have this theory that Sonny does so much pretending he sometimes can't figure out what's real and what's made up.)

Anyway, the Christmas tree is now *way* bigger than me and Sonny, of course. It's, like, two metres tall and growing, growing, growing all the time. It's going to pop out from above the top of the hawthorn trees in a few years' time and blow its cover, if it's not careful. The cemetery gardeners will come with their saws, and me and Sonny and Mum and Dad and Will and Gran and even baby Martha will have to form a protective ring around it, and get the *Islington Gazette* to come along. We'll get them to print the heartwarming tale of how me and Sonny sobbed our two-year-old hearts out (can you believe it?!) when Mum put the Christmas tree out on the street for the bin men to take away one dull January morning, and how Dad went mushy and rescued it, sneaking into the graveyard and secretly planting it in the mini-wood, with me and Sonny helping by pretend-digging and covering ourselves in mud.

The local paper will write all that stuff and then the whole population of Highbury and Islington in North London will all rush to sign our petition to persuade the cemetery owners to give sanctuary to our special tree. . .

Yeah, all that could happen, but never would, 'cause it would all be too horribly embarrassing. I could just imagine Sonny mouthing off, not being able to resist getting some free publicity for himself and mentioning the fact that he was an actor (dahling!!).

"Urgh . . . why are all the males in my family idiots?" I sighed, as I hugged our tree's trunk, and listened to the opening bars of "Last Night" by The Strokes.

TWANNNNGGGG!!

I'd swizzled myself round on the tangy, woody, earth-scented ground and was glancing back though leaves and branches at my ever-noisy house, looking for the source of the latest noise.

At the open window of the room above the garage was a guy in a Radiohead T-shirt pulling faces as he played guitar. *Air* guitar. (Phew for the fact that the only neighbours who could see him were *dead*. . .)

In case you were wondering, the guy in the Radiohead T-shirt was Max, a seventeen-year-old

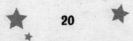

lead guitarist in his head, and my forty-seven-year-old paper-plate salesman dad in real life.

My dad had always been mad about music, and got me and Sonny mad on music too (the rock kind, not Mum's classical stuff), but as we grew up, he'd more or less behaved himself and acted his age. That was back when he'd lived in the main part of the house with me, Mum and my brother. The minute he moved into his ex-office above the garage, he seemed to accidentally drop several decades off his age (oops) and most of his clothes on the floor (picked up, washed, ironed and patiently put away by my mug of a gran whenever she visited).

We called it Dad's BP (Bachelor Pad), and he'd been there for ever. Well, ever since him and mum split up amicably (which is supposed to mean they were both pleased about it, but which *actually* means they just argued in very quiet voices when me and Sonny were around). When that happened, Dad "temporarily" relocated to the room above the garage, till he sorted himself out. In the Dictionary of Dad, "temporarily" seems to mean "permanently". I mean, he hadn't sorted himself out a year or so after he and Mum officially split, when Mum met Will at school (before you barf, Will wasn't a student or anything creepy like that; she was a music teacher and he was a PE teacher). And he *still* hadn't sorted himself out by the time Will moved in six months later.

Then he promised he'd "definitely" get something sorted when Mum told him she was going to have Will's baby. But Dad's version of "definitely" obviously meant "maybe", and so there he was, with flowers and champagne and congratulations, when Mum and Will brought Martha home from the hospital.

My half-sister Martha was now six months old, and as far as I could make out, Dad was going nowhere fast. I mean, I loved him, and I loved having him so near, but it was a freaky situation, right? Specially now, seeing him there, framed in the window of the extension, playing air guitar like he was a saddo teen metal-head, while two windows away (Sonny's room), I could make out Will swooping back and forth, like the hoover junkie he was.

Basically, Dad really, *really* should've been doing what other split-up dads did, and have the decency to move out to a place of his own, somewhere that me and Sonny (unfortunately) could visit.

And one person who'd absolutely *love* for that

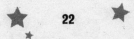

to happen was another of the idiot males in my family: Will.

Will was very nice (there goes that corny word again), even though he used the word "cool" way too often. When he got together with Mum, he was young enough to never seem like a dad-replacement to me and Sonny (get this: he's Mum's toy boy, by ten years!), and sussed enough to never resent Dad staying in the room above the garage.

Ha.

That *last* point was the bit that proved he was as much of an idiot in his own way as my dad. It's, like, of *course* Will minded. He'd have had to be a total *android* not to mind. It didn't matter how many times he casually shrugged off the living arrangements to my laid-back, let's-all-be-friends mum, or how many times he tried to convince me and Sonny that he was completely "cool" with mum's ex living ten centimetres away. We all knew (OK, so *I* knew) that Will was just pretending very, very hard. He could've got a scholarship to Sonny's stupid stage school with his acting skills, when it came to the topic of Dad living too close for comfort. He'd probably end up giving himself an ulcer with the strain of all that secret resentment. And that wouldn't be too "cool" at all.

But forget my dad, the throwback teenager, and Will, the fake "everything's cool!" guy; the prize for Male Idiot in my family had to go to Sonny.

Sonny Bird.

Sonny Bird, star of numerous West End musicals, gazillions of TV roles, and the focus of abundant offers from Hollywood. In his *dreams*.

Sonny got his place at stage school based on lots of kiddie acting roles in local North London drama societies, and the big breaks were yet to come (i.e., all in his head). In the meantime, I had to put up with him practising ballet high-kicks (in the kitchen), singing scales in the shower where the warm air helped his voice (while I was desperately waiting my turn, just to get *clean*), and acting out Shakespeare roles in front of an adoring audience (Dog and Clyde, if no one else was around to suffer).

Sometimes I reminded Sonny of a statistic I once read that only one-in-a-gazillion actors ever make it – the vast majority have to be waiters or sell double glazing or do a whole heap of normal jobs while they keep their fingers crossed and hope for a starring role that never comes. But instead of forcing him to get real, Sonny would just go starry-eyed and come back with stuff like, "And why can't that one-in-a-gazillion be *me*?".

Sigh. . .

Anyway, thank goodness for the females in the family.

Then again, there were times when I tried talking to Mum and she looked at me blankly, 'cause I knew she was busy listening to some eighteenth-century soundtrack in her head instead of me. And Gran was great but, like I said, a bit of a mug when it came to her "little boy" (ho ho – Dad's bachelor diet of takeaways and beer meant nothing about him could be described as "little" any more, specially his stomach). Well, at least Martha rocked (all right, she screamed).

"Hey – it's me!" said Hannah, suddenly wriggling through the space in the garden railings to join me.

"Got bored of your homework, then?" I asked the top of her head, as she ducked expertly under branches so that they didn't muss up her permanently-straightened hair.

"Mmmm. Your mum said she thought you were out here." Hannah folded her cropped-jeaned legs under her as she settled down next to me. "You OK?"

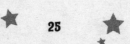

I shrugged, fiddling with a bit of bark in my fingers. "Just thinking about blokes being idiots."

Out of the corner of my eye, I could see Hannah nodding. Now the evening sun was glinting through the trees at us, I could also see that her face wasn't the colour it was meant to be.

"Hannah, did you know that bits of your face are blue?" I asked her, pretty sure that she didn't, and marvelling how laid-back/dippy my mum was not to have mentioned it when she'd let my friend into the house just now – as if it might be some new teen trend she didn't want to criticize.

"*Blue?!*" shrieked Hannah. "Harry! I'll *kill* him!"

Her brother Harry seemed to think that his purpose in life was to bug anyone in his family who was unfortunate enough to be called Hannah.

"The little creep! He grabbed my face and kissed me when I was leaving. I thought *that* was disgusting enough to be the wind-up. I didn't know he had *paint* or something on his hands!!"

And thanks to the blue kiss, Harry could join this evening's role-call of idiot males who long-suffering people like me and Hannah were supposed to love, according to some unfair family rules that someone somewhere made up a long, long time ago.

Dring-dring!! Dring-dring!! my mobile suddenly trilled out, in its old-fashioned telephone mode.

"Text from Letty," I told Hannah, though I knew she wouldn't be too interested. "She wants me to play tennis with her at Highbury Fields tomorrow morning. Snore."

Snore to the fact that tennis was the dullest game in the universe (I *thwack* the ball to you, you *thwack* the ball to me, I *thwack* the ball to you, we do it a lot till someone dies of boredom and the other one wins), and snore to the fact that Letty probably just wanted to hang out at the Highbury Fields tennis courts 'cause a certain Stefan Yates might be there.

"Sounds amazingly dull," said Hannah, spitting into a tatty tissue she'd pulled from her pocket and scrubbing at her face with it. "Still, you can't go, anyway. Not with that other stuff you've got to do."

"What other stuff?" I frowned at her.

She narrowed her eyes at me, which would've been unnerving if her face wasn't blue.

"What?" I repeated, all innocence.

"I *knew* you were fibbing when we were emailing earlier! I *knew* you were just pretending to have something on tomorrow morning to get out of shopping with me."

Hannah's very intuitive, she really is.

"Oh," I mumbled, suddenly remembering my little white on-line lie.

Hannah shrugged. "Whatever,"

Did I mention my friend is very intuitive *and* forgiving?

"So is this stuff coming off?" she asked, switching subjects suddenly. "'Cause I don't want to go back into your house and get laughed at by Sonny and Kennedy."

It was my turn to narrow my eyes at Hannah.

"Better wipe that blue thumb-print off your nose, then," I told her.

"Humph," Hannah fumed, scrubbing more specifically. "So what is going on with Sonny and Kennedy, anyway? When I was walking through the house just now, I heard them laughing in the living room, and Sonny was saying something about you and your *pants*. . ."

Blah. . .

Fine, I texted immediately back to Letty. *What time?*

Tennis might be boring, but it had its advantages. I could pretend the luminous green ball was Sonny's head, after all.

Thwack. . .!

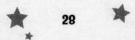

Q: Is this fun? A: No.

Three pairs of Converse trainers padded along the pavement.

The perfect pink pair belonged to Hannah. She was wearing them with a pair of loose, cropped white trousers and a fuchsia-pink T-shirt that said "The Clash" on it. The Clash were a sort of punk-ish band back in the 1970s (a HUGE favourite of my dad's).

Hannah didn't really care who The Clash were, and looked kind of glassy-eyed when Dad once tried to play her one of their most famous tracks "I Fought The Law". The thing is, Hannah loves logo'd tops with the names of classic bands on them, but she's not very fussed about what the classic bands *sound* like.

"Shouldn't be allowed. . ." my dad always grumbles, whenever she wears one of her T-shirts. It kind of annoys me too, but then you can't like your friends one hundred per cent. They're

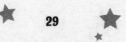

always going to do *something* that bugs you, same as you probably always do something that bugs *them*, like, er, make obvious tap-tapping noises on your computer when they're trying to tell you about their latest Fantasy Boyfriend over the phone. . .

Speaking of Letitia, she was the owner of the green, high-top Converse trainers. She was wearing them with two stupidly long, dark-skinned legs and the shortest denim miniskirt in the world. Thank goodness she wasn't into thongs, that's all I can say.

The scruffy black and white pair of low-rise trainers belonged to me. I wore them with the heels tucked in, for maximum ease of slipping on and off. Yes, I am a very, very lazy person indeed.

"Well," began Letitia, swinging her tennis racket in a very professional-looking way, despite the fact that she'd done plenty of shot-missing and a lot of awkward bending down for balls in her very short mini. "That was fun, wasn't it?"

The answer, plainly, was no.

"It was OK." I shrugged, figuring a half-lie was better karmically than a downright lie.

You know, this morning really *hadn't* been a whole lot of fun. For a start, Letty hadn't been ultra thrilled to see Hannah tagging along with me when we met up, and Hannah was still slightly huffy with me for choosing snores-ville tennis with Letty over total-torture shopping with *her*. I still hadn't figured out why Hannah had decided to tag along this morning (though it was probably just a case of "why not?"), and I still hadn't figured out why people liked playing tennis so much (*boy*, that ball stings when it catches you unawares – there was going to be a *maximum* bruise on my thigh tomorrow, for sure).

"Um . . . he *did* look at me a few times, didn't he?"

When she said that, Letitia blushed, which meant her smooth brown skin went slightly darker. She wasn't just blushing at the memory of Stefan; she was blushing 'cause she didn't want to reveal her innermost lusts to Hannah, but couldn't help herself.

"Yeah, I guess he did," I answered her, telling the truth, but not in the way Letty reckoned it to be.

"Good. . ." said Letty in a small, sweet, smiley way, chocolate-brown eyes open very wide, as she hovered at the road that lead to her house. "Catch up with you later?"

"Sure." I smiled back.

"See you," said Hannah, politely but blankly.

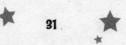

"See you," Letty said, equally politely and blankly to Hannah.

"He was laughing at her, wasn't he?" whispered Hannah, half-a-second after Letty turned off into her street.

I nodded. "Absolutely."

Stefan Yates and his mate had been looking at Letty all right; they checked her out every time she squatted down in a careful wobble and struggled to tug her scrap of denim over her bum as she picked up all the runaway balls. Tragically, she'd looked a bit like she was going to the loo. The way he was sniggering, I don't think Stefan Yates was in any way overcome with longing for her.

Poor Letty; I could've cringed for her. As for Stefan Yates, he was a moron and he didn't know it, so I had to pity him too, in a way.

"Yay – check it out, Sadie! Someone's looking at your poster!" said Hannah, suddenly grabbing my arm and tugging me across the road while there was a gap in the traffic on Highbury Grove. She was talking about a poster I'd knocked together this morning, when I'd found myself in a fug of boredom post-breakfast and pre-tennis.

I'd been stroking Dog, and idly gazing out of my bedroom window (the next smallest room in

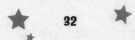

the house, after Martha's), and saw an old notice on a lamp post. I knew roughly what the notice said: "Lost cat – fat and cuddly, answers to Splodge, call blah, blah, blah if any sightings". The notice was ancient and tatty, and our neighbour's cat Splodge had been back home – a little thinner, a little less keen on wandering off – for weeks now. But in my twisted head, it pinged off an idea. . . And ten minutes later, and thanks to a download off the Whipsnade Wildlife Park site, I had an excellent made-up "Lost" poster to pin up and get the unsuspecting public frowning over.

And right now, the unsuspecting public happened to be. . .

"Gran!" I called out, recognizing her stiff-with-hairspray blonde crop, and the glint of her silver specs. From the navy-checked buggy she was pushing a pair of pink arms waved happily.

"Would you look at this nonsense!" said Gran, pointing to the poster I'd carefully pinned up on the tree next to the zebra crossing. "Who'd waste their time with this silliness?"

"What's that, Gran?" I asked, all innocence.

"Just listen!" she continued in her brusque Irish accent. "'Lost – elephant called Bob. If found, call. . .' Now, will you look at that phone number, it's *far* too long. This *has* to be a joke."

Duh. . . It was the *phone number* that gave it away?! Er, not the fact that there was a picture of a large elephant staring back down at her?!

I couldn't look round at Hannah – out of the corner of my eye I could see her shoulders shaking like she was ready to explode.

"Hi, baby!" I said instead to Martha, to take my attention away from Gran's befuddlement and Hannah's infectious shoulder-shudders.

Martha cooed happily up at me. She loved nothing more than going out for long walks with Gran, and Gran loved nothing more than being with her youngest grandchild, even though – and you don't need to be a rocket scientist to figure this out – they weren't *technically* related. (Is there a proper term for what they were? I don't think even step-gran/step-grandkid covers it. . .)

"Ah, now, Sadie," said Gran, turning her attention from the "possibly" fake poster to me. "Just when I was leaving home –" I love the way she calls our place "home", even though she actually lives a good few tube stops further north, in a very nice and hyper-neat bungalow in High Barnet "– I heard your dad asking where you were. He was saying something about wanting to talk to you and Sonny."

What was it, I thought to myself. Did he want

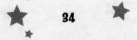

to play us the latest tune he'd not really learned on his imaginary air guitar? Or had he discovered yet another brilliant new band that Sonny and me needed to know about straightaway, if not sooner? Or maybe. . .

"Has he got us tickets to go and see The Drop Zone?" I wondered out loud.

The Drop Zone were being featured as The New Bright Young Things in the music mags that Dad bought, and which me and Sonny nicked from him. Sonny had downloaded their new single, and the three of us were mad for it. Amazingly, they were playing a gig at North London University just up the road from us. Inevitably, it had sold out in five nanoseconds. If Dad had somehow managed to get tickets from somewhere then I'd love him for ever, if I didn't already.

My face was probably a picture of useless hope. Gran and Hannah's were a picture of blankness. (Yeah, right. Two years down the line, when The Drop Zone were humungous, Hannah would be wearing their T-shirt and *still* wouldn't be able to hum you a tune of theirs if you bet her £100.)

"Well, I wouldn't know about that." Gran frowned at me, as if I'd just been talking in Hindustani. "But I do know that he said he was going out somewhere soon, so if you want to catch him, you'd better get yourself moving."

"Later!!" I called out to Hannah. "See you, Gran!"

I started to sprint along the road before Dad vanished – it was absolutely vital that I saw him before he went and left my annoying brother with all the info, and thus a form of torturing me all afternoon ("*Tell* me what Dad said!" "Nope, I don't think so!" "*Tell* me, Sonny!!" "Er, sorry, Sadie, but it's just not going to happen!").

By the way, a tip for other lazy girls who wear their low-rise Converse trainers with the heels tucked in: *always* shuffle in them, *never* sprint. . .

"You all right, Sadie?" I heard Hannah shout.

I couldn't answer her, as I had a mouth full of pavement. . .

An audience of one (rabbit)

As I hobbled towards the house, I was mortified to see that Dad had the *front* window of the garage room open.

The strains of The White Stripes's "Seven Nation Army" was blaring out (excellent!). And – uh-oh – him and Sonny were *yelling* along to the song, framed like the two numpties they were in the open window (*not* excellent. . .).

"Dad!" I hissed, as if he and Sonny could hear me.

("Oooh, that Bird family . . . they're a noisy lot," I could practically hear the neighbours tsking. When they weren't tsking over us for different reasons, that is – like how strange it was that Dad still lived here when Mum had a "new man". Half the street were probably *dying* of curiosity, wondering if Mum and Dad had even got divorced yet. They hadn't.)

Anyway, Dad and Sonny were warbling way

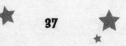

too loudly up in the BP to hear my horrified hissing. So instead I just hurried into the house as fast as my slightly twisted ankle would let me.

"Hi!" I called out to Mum's back, as I passed the living room. She was perched at her piano, with a teetering pile of washing in the laundry basket dumped by her feet. (Mum's piano has strange properties: she regularly gets lured away from whatever she's supposed to be doing by the irresistible magnetic pull of it.)

"Hi, honey! Your dad was looking for you earlier. . ." she said without turning around, and without pausing in the sonata she was plink-plonking through.

"Yep – I know, I saw Gran," I told the back of her head, watching as the dark wavy curls from her loosely piled-up hair bounced in time to the music.

"Good time at the shops?" Mum asked vaguely.

"Tennis courts," I corrected her.

"Buy anything nice?"

Uh-oh; Mum was well and truly lost in music. Sometimes her dippiness was OK (like when Letitia was moaning on about how her mum wanted to know where she was or what she was doing every nano-second of the day), but

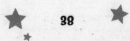

sometimes it could be a bit *arrrrgggghhhh*, if you see what I mean.

Just now, since I was in a rush to speak to Dad, Mum's dippiness was neither OK or *arrrrrgggghhhh*, but somewhere in between. Sort of Ok*aaarggh*.

"Mmm," I mumbled in reply to her as I limped my way away up the stairs, where I went right, and along the corridor to what was once a plain dead-end wall (pre-extension over the garage) and was now the doorway into Dad's BP.

Neither of them spotted me; they were too busy posing in front of an imaginary stadium audience of thousands – while a small house rabbit called Clyde lounged on the bed, staring at them idly.

So I stepped my way over piles of CDs and a plate of dried-in something that might have been last night's tea, and pulled the window shut.

"Hey, hi, Sadie!" Dad beamed, lowering the fictional guitar in his hands.

Urgh. How come I hadn't noticed that he was trying to grow rock dude sideburns? They looked like clumps of sandy-coloured caterpillars stuck to the sides of his face. I didn't think much of the fact that he'd started doing "something" (and I use the term very loosely) with his hair, either. Maybe

Sonny had lent him some of his styling wax, without realizing that it's actually a criminal offence for any male over the age of forty to use stuff like that. Specially when their hair is starting to recede (sorry, Dad, but it's a fact).

"Everyone in the street can hear!" I told them, acting the mum to these two idiot "teenage" boys.

"What's the big deal, Sadie?" Sonny cheekily shrugged at me, but I was pleased to see that he walked across and turned the volume down on the CD player anyway. Wish he hadn't ruffled my hair on the way. Him doing that had bugged me when I was three and it still bugged me now that I was thirteen.

"Sit down . . . chill out," said Dad, shoving a pile of (clean? dirty?) clothes off the bed to make space for me. Clyde bared his sharp little teeth, irked to have been mistaken by Dad for some kind of fluffy T-shirt.

I sat down next to Clyde, but I didn't particularly chill out. My chin and my knee were throbbing too much from my pavement splat two minutes ago and the shame of it was pretty painful too, even if it was only Hannah, Gran, Martha and a few random passing motorists who had witnessed my downfall.

"Here," Dad said next, pulling open his mini-

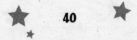

fridge and tossing a can of something cold to me and Sonny simultaneously.

"Gotcha!!" we both called out, catching our Cokes at the exact same split-second. Sonny grinned at me. I sort of snarled back. Dad winked at both of us, chuffed at our synchronicity, even if *I* wasn't.

Dad hadn't done very much to style his BP since he moved in here; he'd added a bed (single), a portable telly (tuned into the VH1 music channel mostly), a two-ring table-top cooker (rarely used), and the minifridge (filled with nutritious beer, plus soft drinks for visitors, i.e. me and Sonny). The tan leather armchair, the band posters, the CD player and mountains of CDs were already here when it was his office. Actually, his office desk was still here too, only now the files had moved to his work unit a couple of streets away and the drawers were filled with his pants and socks (when they weren't strewn on the floor).

Sonny loudly cracked his can open, and sat himself down on the swively office chair. His legs were ridiculously far apart, like those blokes you sometimes have to sit next to on the bus; those guys who seem to be marking their territory by splaying their legs so wide you feel like asking them

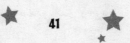

41

if they've got some weird condition like curvature of the hips.

"Why are you sitting like that?" I asked Sonny straight out. It had to be something he'd done in one of his dumb acting classes this week. He was always the same, coming home with a Brooklyn twang, or a melodramatic flourish of his hands, or an annoying click-clack of a tap-dance step, depending on what he'd been up to at stage school that day.

"No reason," Sonny said defensively, immediately reigning his legs in. "Hey, Dad – I forgot to tell you; this new teacher came in to say hi yesterday. He's starting with us next week – his name's Benny. He's amazing: he's a major player in loads of West End musicals."

OK, so this new teacher, Benny, was the one who sat with his legs astride, all macho – Sonny and his sponge of a mind was obviously fixating on him already. And I think what Sonny just said needed to be edited a bit. He'd obviously missed out the words "*used* to be". 'Cause pardon me for being cynical, but if this Benny was *still* a major player in the West End musicals, he wouldn't need to take a job at a North London stage school, and teach people like my big-headed brother and his dorky mate Kennedy stuff, would he? (It just proved that one-in-a-gazillion statistic, didn't it?)

"Great! Good stuff!" said Dad enthusiastically. Still, I guess I'd be pretty enthusiastic too, if I was paying the fearsome fees for Sonny's school. Mucking around doing plays and practising the Riverdance might be fun but it doesn't come cheap. "Anyway, I'm glad I've got you two together—"

"He's into *all* kinds of music," Sonny breezed on, just like he always does. "He said he likes rock and pop, and he really wants to work on some projects with us. He says he's got something pretty exciting in the pipeline."

"That's brilliant! Sounds like a solid guy." Dad nodded, using some of his nicely dated slang that he has no idea is dated. "Anyway—"

"Yeah, and Benny was pretty interested when I said I played guitar, and mentioned all the bands I was into. He'd even heard of The Drop Zone!"

"*Sonny!*" I said sharply, interrupting my brother's flow of verbal diarrhoea. "Dad wants to *tell* us something!!"

Sonny shut up, and nodded, as if he was fine with that and had always meant to shut up at that exact point anyway. And then he crossed his eyes at me, which made me want to giggle *and* ping

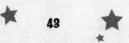

this can of Coke off the side of his stupid head at the same time.

"Well!" said Dad cheerfully, glossing over any niggles between me and Sonny, as per usual. "Here's the thing. . ."

He held up a bunch of leaflet-y looking paper in his hand, which was, I guessed, something to do with "the thing".

"I figured with your mum going back to work next week, it was a good time to move out. So I'm going to check out flats this afternoon!"

So . . . the leaflet-y things were details of places to rent. Wow.

So Dad was finally moving out.

Wow.

Still, what a lame excuse – Mum going back to work after her maternity leave, I mean. Stuff like Will moving in, and Mum having Will's baby – surely you'd think *either* of those would've been a better bet to get him into moving mode. But like I said, Dad's just another useless male, like all the males in my family.

"Um, right," I heard myself muttering aloud. Then I wondered something. "Does Mum know?"

"Not yet," said Dad. "I knew it would affect you two most, so you two are the first to find out!"

Phew – just checking. If Mum had known *that*

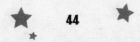

44

little nugget of information and *still* managed to lose herself in her sonata just now, I'd have been seriously worried.

But then my head swivelled back to Dad's news: how did I feel? Well, I guess half of me felt sort of relieved that he was finally making the move and ending our bizarre family living arrangements (the sensible part), and the other half of me was slightly gutted (the five-year-old version of me that kind of wanted to see him every day).

Then I checked out Sonny. Good grief, he wasn't crossing his eyes and goofing around any more. It was as if he'd just heard that Dad had a terminal illness and would be dead by this time tomorrow morning.

Honestly. . .

"It's OK!" said Dad, going over to give Sonny a mannish hug.

In that spare moment, I glanced fondly round the big room, and tried to imagine Dad not being here any more. This airy bright space with no Chili Peppers posters on the walls, no filing cabinets stuffed with old albums he didn't have a player for any more, no pizza boxes on the floor, no Dad. . .

Actually, apart from the no Dad bit, the rest of

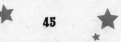

it sounded quite good. This could be a fantastic room to live in, specially since it was slap-bang next to the bathroom (the only part of the main house that Dad currently used, seeing as you could get portable TVs, cooking facilites, minifridges etc. at your local Currys quite easily, but no one had invented a portable, foldaway loo and shower room quite yet).

Anyway, what was that old saying? Every cloud has a silver lining. So if Dad going was the cloud, the silver lining could be me up-sizing from my garden-shed-proportioned bedroom to *this* place.

All it would take was a lick of paint, an industrial hoover to get the three years of pizza crumbs out of the floor, and it would be spectacular.

Goodbye Dad's BP, hello Sadie's space.

"Aw, you don't have to go, do you, Dad?" I heard Sonny muffle into Dad's shoulder.

"Oh, grow up. . ." I grumbled under my breath, thinking that only Clyde could hear me.

Wrong.

Old sonic-eared Sonny had caught that.

"Dad, Sadie said. . ."

The sooner I could move in here the better. With the minifridge and everything, I'd hardly

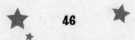

have to come into the main house at all. Though they never said it, I knew Mum and Dad would like it if me and Sonny had a better relationship.

Well, what could be better than us hardly ever seeing each other. . .?

Ooh, what a beautiful dump

"Hmm . . . looks pretty good, huh?"

I swear, my dad is so optimistic that he'd've let an estate agent show him a shipping container with an upturned bin for a table and an ice-cream tub for a sink, and he'd probably say great, yeah, he'd take it.

All I can say is that it was lucky for him I'd offered to trail around and help him check out flats this afternoon. It was unlucky for *me* that Sonny had offered to tag along too.

"Watch this!!" said Sonny, launching himself into a whirl of pirouettes across the large living room.

Groan.

I've got nothing against boys doing ballet. Actually, I like boys doing ballet better than girls doing it; ballerinas tend to flutter about being generally pretty and pink and pathetic, whereas the boys look strong and seriously fit.

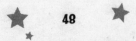

The thing I have something against is Sonny showing off, as usual. This time to a semi-impressed, semi-embarrassed estate agent, who I guess was more used to prospective tenants asking if the cooker was gas or electric than demonstrating their star-turn dancing skills.

"He goes to stage school," I said, by way of explanation.

"*Theatre* school!" Sonny corrected me breathlessly, after all his manic piroutte-ing.

He hated when I called it stage school. To Sonny, it was like calling Leonardo da Vinci a painter and decorator. But I suppose that's why I did it. Annoying Sonny is one of my small pleasures in life.

"Twins, are they?" the estate agent asked Dad, now ignoring me and Sonny as if we were infant school kids, instead of feuding thirteen-year-olds.

Duh. I mean, of *course* we were twins. Did this bloke in the suit and shiny tie *have* to state the boringly obvious? *Yes*, we look very alike: both dark-haired and dark-eyed like Mum, with her olive-y colouring, and both with sort of heart-shaped faces, if you want to describe them that way, though that sounds horribly twee. *Yes*, we have matching thick eyebrows (I need to pluck mine but I'm too scared of pain and of ending up

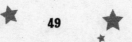

49

with them weirdly wonky-looking). Yes, we both have moles ("beauty spots!" says Gran) above our top lips, on the right. Yes, we're both a bit skinny and gangly (though Sonny's more lean with all the dance training these days, while I'm just plain skinny and gangly). Yes, so we both have slightly lop-sided smiles (Sonny's makes him look like Dopey out of *Snow White*, mine, unfortunately, like I'm snarly, same as *Snow White*'s Wicked Queen).

So yeah, we were *obviously* twins. So why say it?

"Sure are!" said Dad proudly. "Sadie's a whole seven minutes older than Sonny, but who's counting?"

Me, actually. Those seven minutes counted for a lot. Lots of things that don't matter to "single" children matter to twins, like dressing differently and having different friends, and not having people treat you like you're some novelty act.

"Freaky. . ." said the estate agent, glancing from one of us to the other. I wanted to grab the clipboard out of his hand and clip it to his *nose*. And not just for looking at me and Sonny like we were a side-show act from some nineteenth-century circus, but for showing my dad this useless flat.

"We're not *conjoined*, you know," I said out loud, running my hand in the space between me and my brother.

"Sadie. . ." Dad said in a slightly weary, slightly warning voice.

I didn't care if I was being cheeky to a so-called "adult". He was being cheeky to us, calling us freaks. And it was fun seeing the confusion in the bloke's face; it didn't seem like he had any idea what conjoined meant. ("It's the proper word for Siamese twins," I felt like spelling out patronizingly to him, but didn't want another weary, warning look from my normally laidback dad.)

"As you can see, Mr Bird, it's beautifully proportioned accommodation," the estate agent suddenly prattled on, remembering he had a dump to flog.

"Dad, there's no central heating in this place," I butted in, blatantly ignoring the estate agent. "And there's black mould in the bathroom."

"Oh. . ." said Dad sadly, looking around the living room he'd imagined blasting his music out in, as I pointed out the flat's failings.

"And I spotted mouse poo in the kitchen, too," I added, so he could get all thoughts of this big room and surround-sound speakers out of his head.

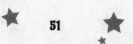

It was the fifth flat we'd looked at, and the fifth flat I'd had to force him into a reality check over.

"Nice!" Dad had nodded, looking round Flat No. 1.

"Nice and handy for the train," I'd pointed out – very loudly – as the two-thirty to King's Cross thundered by a couple of metres from the window, shaking the whole house.

"It's . . . cosy!" Dad had said about Flat No. 2.

"Dad, it's smaller and less comfy than our *car*!" I told him.

"It's got a whirlpool bath!" Sonny had yelped, when he'd gone exploring Flat No. 3.

"And it looks like it's got a drug den next door," I shuddered, pointing to the shifty-looking guy leaving the flat along the landing, where an equally shifty-looking guy was peering at us through a slit in the door, and wrestling with his snarling pit bull to stop it from escaping.

"Wow, the acoustics are amazing!!" Dad had said, clapping his hands for echo effect in the chunk of converted warehouse that was Flat No. 4, with Sonny nodding enthusiastically by his side.

"Yeah, and the rent's so steep you'd have to take Sonny out of stage school to pay for it!" I mentioned, half-hoping he might actually *take* the flat for that very reason. . .

"Oh, well. Maybe we'll see something *next* weekend," Dad had said resignedly, plopping the bunch of flat details into the nearest bin as we traipsed along the pavement, headed back home. "And I'm sure Mum and Will will be able to put up with me for a little bit longer!"

Yeah, Will wouldn't mind at all. And I'm a fabulously attractive rhinoceros.

"Hey, look at the time," said Dad, glancing at his watch. "Think the guys from work were planning on going down the pub this afternoon to watch the Arsenal match. I might drop down there for a bit."

Aargh . . . how could he do this to me? It would still take another ten minutes to walk home, alone with Sonny. No thanks.

"Whatever," I said, thinking on my feet. "I'm just going to go and get a magazine."

"Shall I wait for—"

"Nope," I called back to Sonny as I stepped into the sanctuary of the newsagent we'd been passing.

Ten minutes of Sonny drivelling on about stage school and auditions and what his idiot mate Kennedy was up to – it would be like losing ten minutes of my life. . .

*

Family conversations – they just sometimes bore you to death, don't they?

As soon as I walked back in the house, and through to the kitchen, I was so instantly bored by what I heard that I felt like carrying on straight out of the back door, straight through the hole in the railings and into the cemetery. At least all my dead friends out there didn't witter away endlessly.

"I just worry, that's all," Mum was saying, sitting at one side of the kitchen table.

"But what's there to worry about?" Will replied, bouncing Martha on his knee.

Mum and Will were doing this same back-and-forth chat that they'd been having since way before Martha was even born. I should've just recorded them doing it and played it out loud half-a-dozen times a day to save them the bother.

"I keep thinking that she's just so little for me to be starting back at work already. . ." sighed Mum.

"It'll be cool! After all, it's not as though someone *else* is going to be looking after her – *I* am, remember!" Will was trying to sound calm and soothing, but I could tell by the way the bouncing was getting more agitated that he was probably as bored of this months-old conversation as me. And I guess it was a bit like Mum saying she didn't think he was up to it.

Luckily, Martha was loving the frantic bouncing and was giggling happily to herself. I sat down in the chair closest to her and reached out to tickle her bare toes.

"But—"

"Mum," I cut right in, dying to help wrap up this dead-end subject and get on to more important things, like if I could get Dad's room when he moved out. "You earn *lots* more than Will. You're *head* of the music department at your school. Will *offered* to be a stay-at-home dad, remember? It makes sense. You both talked about it and decided on this *ages* ago."

I know it sounds like I was being bossy. But Mum is such a daydreamer that if you don't yank her back to reality sometimes, she'll twitter around in ever-decreasing circles till she gets her own head – as well as everyone else's – all in a spin. And she never minds me talking to her like this; in fact, during a little speech she gave for me and Sonny's birthday last year, she looked lovingly at me and described me as the rock of the family: the sensible one, the dependable one, the one that was "endlessly capable". Yeah, endlessly capable of being sensible, dependable and rock-like. Fantastic. *Exactly* what a non-singing, non-dancing, non-acting twelve-year-old girl wants to hear when her twin has just been accepted at stage school and his parents told by the headteacher that his "boundless talent and great charm and enthusiasm will be an asset to the school"...

"Mmm, you're right, Sadie." Mum now nodded, gazing at me with anxious eyes. "It's just that Martha seems so small and helpless..."

The small and helpless Martha chose that exact second to happily barf up a bunch of milky gloop all down her chin and all over Will's hands.

"Yeah, you must be really gutted at the idea of missing out on all *this*!" I teased Mum, as I automatically grabbed a handful of Wet Wipes from the pack on the table and swiped Martha and Will clean again.

"I guess it'll be tough!" Mum laughed, I was pleased to see.

Phew. Now I could get down to business (*room* business) while Sonny wasn't around, and before the idea of asking for Dad's room occurred to *him*.

"Listen, Mum, now that Dad's moving out—"

The end of the sentence never happened. Gran dropping the loaded washing basket on the mat by the back door made us all jump. But in that slo-mo second before it went clattering, I spotted the surprised expressions on Mum and Will's faces (and the utterly shocked look on Gran's) and suddenly remembered that they had no idea of Dad's imminent plans.

"Joan!! Are you OK?" said Mum, jumping up and rushing over to Gran, who was holding her hand over her mouth, as if I'd just announced that Dad had robbed a bank or run off with a nun or something.

"He's just trying to rent a flat somewhere round Highbury!" I said quickly, in case Gran thought he was moving to a shanty town in Buenos Aires.

But it was too late to console Gran – I guess she was worried that Dad finally moving out meant she'd have no excuse to pop to ours every second day.

"Joan – come and sit down, I'll get you a cup of tea," said Will, jumping up and ushering her towards the table. I could have sworn that as well as that frown of concern there was a faint smile of relief going on. He was probably *dying* to ask me for more details.

"Um, that's all I know. Dad'll tell you later. I'll take Martha," I mumbled hurriedly, scooping my little sister from Will's arms so he could help

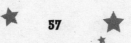

Mum calm Gran. I'd help by being "dependable" and looking after Martha – while avoiding a cross-examination by my slightly hysterical gran.

As I stepped out into the sunny garden, I felt a rub of fur as Clyde appeared and followed me out of the madhouse. Dog was sprawled in a sunny patch of lawn, which seemed like an excellent place for us all to be. I plonked me and my pleasantly uncomplicated baby sis down next to her.

Martha gurgled happily, trying to reach for a handful of Clyde's fur. I expertly moved her away so she could grab handfuls of grass instead, which wouldn't growl at her.

"I didn't mean to upset anyone. I just wanted to ask about the room," I mumbled, tousling Martha's dandelion-soft tufts of blonde hair. "But anyway, knowing Dad, *you'll* probably be sixteen by the time he *finally* moves out. . ."

I glanced back at the house, to see how the calming was going on. Fair hair, dark hair, silvery-blonde hair, all bent together in chatter around the kitchen table. My concerned sort-of-stepdad, my comforting mum, my distraught gran.

Maybe since none of them were looking, I could finally take Martha somewhere she'd never been yet.

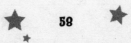

"Want to meet some dead people?" I asked her cheerfully, thinking that now was a good time to introduce my little sister to my special place, under the Christmas tree. I wasn't scared of breaking her or anything, but Martha'd been so small up till now that I hadn't fancied squishing her through the rusty railings and risking pine cones thunking on her delicate little head. But now she seemed stronger, and had a tubby baby fat layer to protect her. (In her nappy, she looked like a very cute miniature sumo wrestler.)

Dring, dring! Dring, dring!

I'd just started to pick Martha up from the grass, but immediately had to lower her back down to answer my mobile.

"Hey, Sadie!" said a bright, breezy and very annoying voice.

"Where are you?" I asked my brother, wondering if he'd got lost on the way home. (Hey, a girl can dream.)

"I just left Dad's new flat!"

"What! What d'you mean?" I said, trying to hide my shock, since I knew Sonny would love that.

"Well, after you went to the newsagent, I walked down the road a bit with Dad, and we saw this sign for a flat to rent in a shop window."

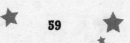

"And?"

This was bliss to Sonny, merrily telling me something I had no idea about.

"And so we went to see it. And it's brilliant. He's put down a deposit and everything. He's moving in next weekend."

"So? Where is it?"

"Not telling."

"Don't be stupid. Where is it?"

"Nope. Dad can get the keys again tomorrow – he wants to show you it then."

"Yeah, well, that's great, but why can't you tell me about it now?"

"It's a surprise."

What could be so surprising about a flat? Was it made of *gold*?

"Don't be stupid. Put Dad on," I ordered him, trying to sound like his older (by seven minutes) sister, and determined to get some sense out of someone.

"Can't. He's gone to watch that football match in the pub. There's no point phoning him there – it's too noisy and he won't hear it. Anyway, he won't tell you because he wants it to be a surprise."

I hate the word "glee"; it's one of those words that's so sugary you feel like you've eaten twenty

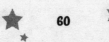

profiteroles in a row and feel sick when you say it. Or maybe that's just me.

But my annoying brother was positively bursting with glee at keeping a secret from me.

I'd have to punish him. Maybe I could give Clyde his tea early and then lock him in Sonny's room without a litter tray.

"Whatever," I said, feeling about as far from a casual "whatever" as it's possible to get.

"*Meeeoooooooow!!*"

I threw my phone down on the grass without a bye, as I rushed to extract Dog from the loving vice-like grip of Sumo Baby. . .

Yewww...

"So me and Kennedy, we're working on this improvisation thing in drama class, right?" said Sonny.

Mum, Dad, Will and Gran all nodded, intrigued. Martha waved a teaspoon around and accidentally walloped herself on the head. I yawned.

"So we're both supposed to be, like, *gang* members, and we're having a fight like this, right?"

How bizarre. Against a backdrop of deep pink walls and myriads of jewel-coloured Turkish glass lamps and intricate tiles, my doofus of a brother stood up and re-enacted a one-sided punch-up with an invisible opponent. The waiters and the other customers of the Iznik café looked pretty startled.

I wished he'd shut up and sit down. I wished my family wouldn't encourage him.

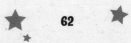

"Then Kennedy gets me in a headlock, yeah?"

Urgh. Now he looked like he was auditioning for *The Hunchback of Notre Dame*. Why did he feel he had to *share* everything with us all the time? I didn't try to bore my family and any other poor, innocent bystanders by reciting my most recent geography lesson to them, did I?

"And then I throw *Kennedy* off like *this*. . ."

Kennedy. Now there really *is* a doofus. He's kind of wide without being fat, if you see what I mean. He's the kind of guy who'd get signed up in a second to be in a school rugby squad 'cause if he ran at the opposite team with his elbows out, he'd take four players down at once, like a human steamroller. But he's wide all over, with this wide head and this wide grin, which makes his face sound like a friendly-looking plate. But that Cheshire Cat grin of his is just the window-dressing for someone with a moronic sense of humour. He's just one of those laughing-*at*-you kind of people, never-*with*-you.

And another thing about Kennedy: his real name's Kenneth. But the bigwigs in charge at the stage school thought Kenneth was a bit of a lame name and suggested he changed it to Kennedy on the stupid cards that get send out to casting directors with your face (big, *wide* face, if you're

Kennedy) splashed all over them. Sonny has one of those cards, naturally. The main photo is of him doing this star jump in mid-air, and sort of shouting. Wow, it's so cheesy.

Anyway, the thing that gets me is that the stage school whoevers said he needed a new stage name for his *card*, right? So why did he have to start calling *himself* "Kennedy" too? And why did he insist everyone else had to as well, including his mum and dad? I mean, how naff is that?

"And then so I say to Kennedy, '*I* is the main man round here. . .'"

Help. I couldn't take one more excruciating second of this. Dad had taken us all out for Sunday lunch at our family's favourite fancy café to celebrate him getting a new place of his own, but it was turning into less of a treat now that Sonny was prattling on and endlessly *on*. (Not that Gran seemed to be enjoying her treat too much – she's more of a shepherd's pie kind of girl. Shish kebab and couscous slightly frighten her.)

"Dad – I think maybe we should make a move. There're people waiting for a table," I said, interrupting Sonny's monologue.

Now, *that* was a good one. We'd been finished with our meals for a while (all except Gran, who

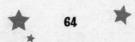

was nibbling at a falafel like it was a witchetty grub or a potentially fatal poisonous fruit from the deepest Amazonian rainforests), and there genuinely *was* a family hovering hopefully by the door, scanning the room for people wrapping up their lunches.

What I'm saying is, it didn't sound at all like I'd deliberately and rudely interrupted Sonny because he was being a big fat bore. Which of course I *was* doing and he *was* being.

"Oh, oh, right. Yep, I'll ask for the bill," said Dad, taking my point on board. The rest of the family started doing a getting-ready-to-go fidget; all except Sonny, who shot me an I-know-what-you-just-did scowl.

Well, served him right for hanging on to the secret of Dad's new BP for the last twenty-two hours. (Not that I was counting.)

Speaking of which. . .

"So, can we go and check out the flat now, Dad?" I asked, standing up and swinging Martha up out of the highchair she was in, and getting my cheeks slapped with chubby, hummus-covered hands for my trouble.

"Sure!" Dad said, rummaging in his wallet for cash. "Are you good to go, Sonny?"

What?!

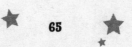

"Yep!" said Sonny enthusiastically.

Nooooo!!

Why did Sonny have to come too? He'd already seen the place, hadn't he? Did he just want to stand and stare at my reaction, when I saw whatever was supposed to be surprising about it? Uh-oh, that made me worried. Dad's new BP must be *seriously* bad. Will had better wipe that contented look off his face, 'cause if it was lousy, then chances were, Dad might be knocking at our front door in a couple of weeks' time, with his stuff in a bin bag and his eye on the garage room again.

And then I'd *never* get the chance to move into it. . .

It had to be a joke.

An *undertakers*?!

"Actually, I think they like to be called funeral directors," Dad said cheerfully, standing hands on hips outside the black-glossed frontage of "McConnell & Son". The lettering was in antique gold, just like you'd expect. For a second, I wondered if any groovy young undertakers had ever thought of going wild and bucking the trend; having shopfronts painted the same vivid pink as the inside of the Iznik café maybe, with cheery people standing outside, handing out multicoloured balloons with logos like: "Smile!! Being Dead's Not So Bad!"

Then I got real and thought about the fact that Dad was going to be living in a flat above dead people.

"Are you mad?" I asked Dad. Sonny stood at his side, just grinning.

"What?" said Dad, in mock surprise. "I thought you'd think it was pretty amazing, Sadie! I mean, you love that old cemetery behind the house, don't you?"

Yes, I did. The difference was, the cemetery behind the house was full of anciently dead people who were probably just harmless and organic dust by now. The difference was, the people behind the shopfront here were very *newly* dead people. Now *that* was creepy.

"Dad, how can you drink beer and play air guitar in your flat, knowing there're . . . y'know . . . *bodies* downstairs?" I asked him, as he strode towards the door to the right of the shopfront and put the key in the lock.

"I'll just try not to think about it, and console myself with the fact that this place is twice as big and costs a third less than practically anything we saw yesterday afternoon." He smiled over his

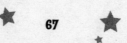

shoulder at me as he began stomping up the nondescript stairs.

"What till you see it; it *is* big," said Sonny, coming up the stairs behind me. "You can do cartwheels in the living room!"

I rolled my eyes, absolutely sure that that's exactly what Sonny had done yesterday afternoon when he came to look at it with Dad.

But yeah, he was right. It was huge. Through the flat's front door, there was a hall that was practically the same size as my bedroom (i.e., big for a hall, titchy for a bedroom). The empty room at the front, overlooking the busy street and perched over the "McConnell & Son" sign, was so wide I thought it was the living room, but nope – it was the bedroom.

"Just going to road-test my new loo!" Dad grinned, heading into the bathroom and closing the door.

"Check this out!" said Sonny, waving me through to the living room at the back.

"*Please* don't let him do any cartwheels now," I muttered under my breath, as I walked through into the massive empty room, with its bare white walls and plain, sandy carpet. The light spilled in through a large window – and a glass door, strangely enough.

"Where does that go to?" I asked, walking across and trying the metal handle. It opened easily.

"It's a fire escape down to the yard," Sonny's voice drifted behind me.

And now I heard a different voice floating up from somewhere below.

I peeked out, and saw the top of a very red head of hair. A man, or maybe a boy (it was hard to tell from this angle), was sitting halfway down, or halfway up (depending on your perspective), the dark green painted metal stairs.

He was talking to himself.

Uh-oh.

". . .here's one for you: Why do birds fly south for the winter? 'Cause it's too far to walk!"

Hmm. Was he telling himself a *joke*? OK, let's call it a *non*-joke, since it wasn't very funny.

"And hey – what did the zero say to the number eight? 'Nice belt!'."

I got it; not the non-joke, I mean,

I mean, the fact that *maybe* this guy had on one of those mobile headsets, and was telling his non-jokes to someone *else*. (Poor them.)

"Then there was this schoolkid who put his lunch money in a vending machine so he could buy some sweets. The vending machine said, 'Oi! You'll get fat eating that rubbish!' And the kid

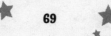

says to his mate, 'This machine's *well* out of order!'."

Boom boom.

This guy was hilarious, I don't think.

And uh-oh . . . he'd just turned his head this way and that – as if he was looking round at a non-existent audience – giving me the chance to see that there was no mobile-phone headset in sight. Great. Dad apparently had a neighbour who was certifiably mad. I knew there had to be a drawback to this vast, cheap flat. Apart from the bodies lurking downstairs, of course.

"What's—"

"Shush!!" I tried to shut Sonny up as he came over to stick his nosey nose out of the fire escape door. But those voice projection lessons at stage school had worked too well, and so of course the red-headed crazy person turned to look up. OK, so he was more of a crazy teenage boy, now I could see his freckly face properly. He was about seventeen-ish, maybe.

"Er . . . hi!'" he said, blushing a fuchsia shade of pink.

"Hi," me and Sonny said in unison, which I really, *really* hate doing. It's like the times we accidentally sort of finish each other's sentences ("Sadie, have you seen my—", "Yeah, you left your

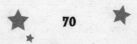

iPod next to Martha and she's using it as a teething ring, you muppet."). It's all way too cosily *twinny*, if you see what I mean.

"I'm . . . um . . . Cormac. I . . . uh . . . live up there," said the boy, pointing to the floor above Dad's and coming up the stairs awkwardly, as if his jeans were made of stiff cardboard and he was having trouble walking. Or maybe his legs were just as embarrassed as his face and he had a severe case of mortification of the limbs. I had the same thing once when I did a bellyflop in the school swimming pool and then had to walk with reluctant legs past the whole of the jeering boys in my class. But that was hardly the same; I was just a humiliated girl in pain, not a psychopath who told jokes out loud to no one.

"I'm Sadie, he's Sonny and our dad's moving in here," I mumbled hurriedly in reply, wondering how quickly I could retreat and close this stupid fire escape door.

"Hey, what were you doing?" Sonny asked straight-out, with a big grin. (Had he no shame? And didn't he know it was dangerous to provoke the mentally deranged?!)

"Um . . . well, I was just practising my stand-up routine."

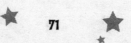

71

"Yeah?" said Sonny, all interested. "Stand-up – so you mean you do comedy?"

No, he most certainly did not. Hadn't Sonny heard those lame so-called jokes just now?

"S'cuse me, I've just got to go and . . . *do* something. . ." I muttered, leaving them to it. I swear, Sonny would've struck up a conversation with a serial axe murderer, if he thought they had a love of performance in common. (Serial Axe Murderer: "You know, I find it strangely soothing to recite the sonnets of John Donne as I hack my victims to death." Sonny: "Wow! That's *so* interesting! I like to practise songs from *Grease* when *I'm* in a bad mood!")

I needed to go and hang out with someone bearable and vaguely sane. Unfortunately, there was no one around like that, so Dad would have to do.

I found him in the front room, lying splayed on the polished wood floor, eyes closed. I might have worried he'd collapsed or something, if he hadn't been singing the Kaiser Chiefs' old song "Oh My God"; the one that goes on about never having been this far away from home. I guess it was kind of appropriate.

"Ah, great!" he said, breaking off from his tuneless warbling. "Here, Sadie – catch!"

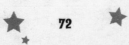

I caught it – "it" being a piece of white chalk he'd just chucked at me.

"What's this for?"

"Draw round me. I want to see if this would be a good place for my bed. Then I'm going to draw in where I'm going to put the giant free-standing speakers I'm going to buy, so I can listen to music in bed."

"No way!" I told him. "It'd look like one of those scene-of-the-crime things, where the police have traced an outline of the body of whoever's been killed!"

"Don't be so morbid, Sadie!" Dad laughed, pushing himself up on his elbows and grinning at me.

"Says the man who's chosen to live above an undertaker!!" I pointed out, folding my arms and raising my eyebrows at him.

And what did he have to say to that? Nothing; instead, he just burst into a rousing chorus of "Live Forever" by Oasis. Now, I know I love music, but not when it's my dad doing the singing.

"See you back at the house," I said, putting my fingers in my ears.

As I closed the flat's front door, I could hear him singing some new song about needing some "BODY!!" to love.

It was a shame to waste the piece of chalk I was still holding.

"BEWARE!" I wrote neatly on the grey wall by the door. "MEN OF VERY LITTLE BRAIN INSIDE. SPEAK SLOWLY AND DO NOT EXPECT ANY SENSE."

Job done, I set off home to hang out with the more intuitive, sensitive and infinitely more intelligent members of my family, who happened to be a six-month-old baby, a very patient cat and a slightly grumpy rabbit. . .

Sonny and the strange "whatever"

Standing in front of the long mirror, I held the burgundy cord jacket up against me. It was great, and it was cheap, and I really wanted it.

It was just a pity it was four sizes too big and smelled a bit whiffy.

"Do you remember Westlife?" Letitia suddenly asked, sucking in the pink balloon of bubblegum she'd just blown.

"Nope," I said, hanging the jacket back on the rail.

Of course I did.

It's just that there're two sorts of music I don't like: classical (sorry, Mum, I just don't get it) and cheesy boy band stuff. Me, Dad and Sonny *hate* those retro *I ♡ the '90s* sort of shows that ignore all the good music from the decade and show video clips of corny-looking guys singing lame covers instead. We even once talked about setting up a website called "Boybands'r'Pants", but we didn't bother, 'cause, thankfully, boy bands aren't around as much as they used to be. Phew.

"My sister used to love Westlife. When I was little, she had posters of them all over her bedroom walls." Letitia continued chatting, as I continued mooching around the second-hand clothes shop we'd come to after school.

"Which sister?" I asked, which was a dumb question, really (it *had* to be Kelise, who was eighteen, 'cause Charonna was only four, and her favourite song ever was "The Wheels On The Bus"). And I guess it was a dumb question because I was only really half listening to Letty, to be honest.

"Kelise. Anyway, when I thought about her old posters last night, I realized that Stefan looks *exactly* like that blond one in Westlife. Don't you think?"

Weren't they *all* kind of blond in Westlife? I couldn't picture them; when I tried to remember them, their faces all sort of melted into one. They were all like good-looking Mr Potato Heads, I vaguely remembered. I gave silent thanks that I was too young (unlike Kelise) to take much notice of Westlife and other boy bands when they had their hey-day. I was more into Scooby-Doo. I think I'd rather have listened to Scooby-Doo howling than a boy band singing.

"I think he's more like the dark-haired one," I said, just for something to say, so Letty would think I was still joining in with her Stefan Yates conversation. I'd spent the whole of today (Monday) listening to her obsessing over him and I was getting quite good at answering her without really listening too hard. It's amazing how convincing a few well-placed "mmm"s, "yeah"s and nods are.

"*Which* dark-haired one?" Letty frowned at me.

"The taller one," I said, making it up on the spot.

"Do you think so?" Letty said thoughtfully, mulling over my made-up opinion.

Over her shoulder, I noticed something far more interesting than Stefan Yates and his resemblance to a potato-headed boy band member. It was a poster for The Drop Zone, as their gig was happening at the university just up the road from the shop we were in.

My heart gave a flip of excitement at seeing their name, and a flop of misery knowing I wasn't going. I glanced round at a few of the browsing customers, all artfully scruffy students from the uni, and wondered if any of them had a precious ticket for the gig tucked away in their wallets or Filofaxes. Maybe I could throw myself at their

mercy, and beg them to sell me their ticket. I could raise the money to pay for it somehow. Perhaps I could sell something . . . but what could I sell that I wouldn't miss? Of *course*: Sonny. I could probably get quite a lot for him if I sold him as a personal slave. And the added bonus of getting rid of him would be that the house'd be a whole lot less like an outpost of stage school.

"What d'you think?" asked Letitia, suddenly spinning round and showing off the satin top hat that she'd just stuck on at a rakish angle.

"Wear it with your long black winter coat and you'd get a job in that undertaker place Dad's moving in above," I told her, trying to imagine Letty walking very sombrely in front of a carriage drawn by two glossy black horses with dark, feathery plumes wedged into their forelocks.

Nah, she'd just get the giggles.

"Yuck!" Letty shuddered. "If I was you, I'd just refuse to visit him there! It's too creepy if his only neighbours are . . . y'know . . . like, dead or whatever!"

I didn't know what she meant by "whatever". McConnell & Son's clients were pretty much properly dead, I supposed, or they weren't doing their job right.

"There is at least one *live* neighbour," I told her, remembering the non-funny teenage psychopath, who probably wasn't really a psychopath, as he'd blushed a lot and I think deeply mad people are too busy being deeply mad to get embarrassed about people overhearing them tell lame jokes aloud.

"Who's that then?" asked Letty, taking the top hat off and plonking it back on the shelf.

"A guy. He's about seventeen, I think. He lives in the flat upstairs from Dad."

"Oh!" said Letty, in that ears-pricked-up tone of voice she uses when she's hearing about a someone who might be a potential Fantasy Boyfriend for the future.

"Oh, no . . . he's not your type," I said, with a shake of my head, thinking of Cormac's shock of spiky ginger hair and his kind of goofy expression. Letitia only went for very handsome types who were way out of her league. It's not that Letty isn't cute – she is, but she's the sort of thirteen-year-old girl who could easily pass for a twelve-year-old, and she's well under the radar of her Fantasy Boyfriends. Specially when her Fantasy Boyfriends have often been people like one of the presenters on Saturday morning telly, and a male model she spotted once at the Screen On The

79

Green cinema in Islington. (She recognized him out of one of her magazines.)

"Letitia would get very scared and run a mile if anyone actually asked her to be their *real* girlfriend," Hannah said once, in that diggy sort of way. Thing is, I think Hannah might be right.

"Arghhh . . . is that the time?" Letty gasped, glancing at the retro clock on the wall. "I've got to go – I promised Mum I'd pick up Charonna from a playdate."

That sounded pretty non-exciting. Still, I was half-tempted to offer to go with her – it would be more fun than going home, since I knew I'd be walking in on some mean gang warfare (stage school style). . .

"Oh."

"Hi, Sadie. Um, what's up?" asked Will. He was sitting at the table in his PE tracksuit, waving a yellow floppy rabbit in front of Martha, who was paying it no attention at all. Her tiny stomach was on a timer set for tea, and her eyes were gazing at Mum, willing her to stop rummaging in the plastic bag on the table and get on with feeding her. The wailing would start in about, oooh, ten seconds' time.

"It's a bit quiet, that's all," I said, dumping my

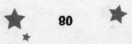

school bag down and glancing around for any signs of the mean gang warfare I'd been expecting. "I thought Sonny said this morning that he was having Kennedy back tonight, so they could practise their stupid gang improvisation thingy?"

"Mmm, he's not home yet," said Mum abstractedly, pulling a floaty, flowery sort of top out of the bag. "Do you like it, Sadie? I just bought myself some new work clothes."

I nodded. "Yeah, it's nice." Mum has OK taste in clothes. Not *my* kind of thing, but she looks pretty good in what she wears.

"Which do you think for my first day, Sadie – *this* one or *this* one?"

Another floaty, flowery top, a lot like the first flowery top.

"That one," I said assuredly, though my choice was about as random as if I'd done "Eeny-meeny-miny-mo, catch a tiger by the toe".

"Yes, you're absolutely right," murmured Mum, staring at the one I'd pointed at, before folding both her new tops away. She looked so dreamily distracted that I suspected she'd have forgotten whichever top I'd chosen by 8.15 a.m. on Monday morning when she was getting dressed.

"So . . . all change from next week, eh, Sadie?" said Will, pushing his fair hair back off his face.

"Your mum'll be back at work, *I'll* be here at home, and your dad'll be . . . at his new place. (". . .and your dad'll be gone, thank goodness," was probably what Will *wanted* to say, but was too tactful to.)

"Yeah." I shrugged, acting like it wouldn't make much difference to me, but I supposed it would be seriously weird. Not so much Mum working, 'cause she'd always done that till Martha turned up, but Will being the stay-at-home dad, and Dad being gone, was both going to take some getting used to.

"It'll be cool." Will nodded, trying to look very sincere and reassuring.

"*WAAAAAAAAAAAAAAAAAAAAAHHHH HH!!!!*"

Told you. As Martha went off like a fire-station siren, Will visibly jumped, swapping the sincere and reassuring expression for one of shock and confusion.

Boy, was he going find being a full-time kiddy-carer fun. Not.

"Hey. . ."

Great, Sonny was home. I should go and grab some earplugs before the excitable twittering started. He'd been going on about that new teacher at the weekend; it would probably be the never-ending topic of today as well.

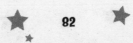

"Hi!" Kennedy roared breezily at us all, then saved a knowing grin for my eyes only, just to let me know he hadn't forgotten the other day and the whole BRA and PANTS yelling thing.

Urgh.

"I'm going to put tea on in a little while. What do you guys fancy?" asked Will, doing his helpful man-about-the-house routine while Mum took Martha for a cuddle while she dumped her shopping bags upstairs out of the way.

"Whatever. . ." said Sonny, slouching off his bag and heading out of the back door and into the garden.

Excuse *me*.

Sonny never said "whatever". Sonny never slouched.

As Kennedy followed my brother outside, like some lolloping Labrador, I swapped a vaguely puzzled glance with Will.

"Seems a bit down?" he suggested, as we heard the thud-thud of a football being hit against the brick wall between our house and the one next door.

"Sonny doesn't get 'down'," I said, slightly flummoxed. "Sonny only does happy. *Annoyingly* happy."

Perhaps he was doing some method acting for

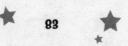

a part at school, rehearsing being a mopey teenager or something.

"Maybe it's 'cause your dad's moving out?" Will speculated. Will's OK. I mean, even if he was personally, deliriously glad that Dad was moving out this weekend, he at least had the decency to wonder if it was making Sonny upset. Which I didn't have. The decency, I mean.

A twinge of guilt made me head out into the garden. I suppose I should be the nice older (by seven minutes) sister for once, and check if Sonny was all right.

"Hi. . ." I began, talking to Sonny's back as he kick, kick, kicked the ball aginst the wall.

"What's up, Sadie?" Kennedy grinned, perching himself on the outdoor rabbit hutch that we were too soft to ever put Clyde into (he preferred to share Dog's basket, as well as litter tray).

"Not much," I answered, without looking at him. "What's up with *you*, Sonny?"

Whack, went the ball.

"Nothing," said Sonny, *almost* monosyllabically.

Something was definitely wrong. Sonny never said just one word when he could come out with seventeen. Even Dog looked concerned – OK, make that annoyed – as she stared down at Sonny from the top of the wall where she'd probably been trying to snooze. Her tail was whacking on the wall, almost in time to the slaps of the ball on brick.

"Um, something bugging you?" I asked, wishing Kennedy wasn't here. Sonny might be pretty good at acting out emotional scenes, but he was a boy, after all, and boys are naturally rubbish at showing they have any kind of feelings in front of other boys. Particularly if they're their best mates.

"Nope," Sonny answered, still keeping his eyes on the ball.

"Hey, Sonny," said Kennedy, a sneaky, teasing grin on his face. "Aren't you going to tell Sadie about that audition for—"

"Leave it, Kennedy!"

A-ha. Maybe Sonny's less-than-sunny mood wasn't down to Dad leaving at all. He was always yacking on about the parts he was constantly auditioning for (kid in a washing powder commercial, kid in the background of *Holby City*, kid "mmmm"ing over horrible breakfast cereal in a TV ad – never the lead part for a *Harry Potter* spin-off series or anything). Maybe he was up for a particularly lame part this time, one that I could legitimately tease him over for the rest of his life. Kid in a diarrhoea cure ad, maybe?

The only thing that stopped me getting stuck

into the remorseless teasing immediately was the fact that I wanted to seem a lot more mature and sensitive than Kennedy.

"Well, if you want to talk or whatever," I said vaguely and uncomfortably, as I turned to go back inside. Maybe Sonny didn't hear me; I hadn't spoken very loudly, and he was back to whacking the ball pretty hard.

"*Yeeeeeeooooooowwwww. . .*"

Swivelling around, I saw a ball – and the cat it had hit – go flying over the wall into next door's garden.

Sonny seemed to have mistaken Dog for a goal, and had just scored 1-0. . .

Nine lives and counting. . .

Bull terriers have the titchiest little eyes in the world, don't they? It's like nature got its paperwork muddled up one day and gave the wrong eyes to bull terriers and bush babies. Think about it; bush babies' eyes are so big, there's hardly any room on their tiny faces for noses and mouths.

Yes, as you may have guessed, I was bored. I'd been sitting in the vet's waiting room this afternoon for a ridiculously long time, and my feeble brain was scrambling around for anything to keep it entertained.

First, I'd tried listening to the radio that was playing on the receptionist's desk, but instead of music it was tuned to a talk station, which is a waste of a radio as far as I'm concerned.

Then I sat thinking about poor Dog (she'd been limping badly ever since Sonny had splatted her off the wall yesterday).

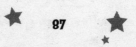

Then I thought about the conversation I'd walked in on after school today.

"Are you sure Max will be fine?" (Gran, fretting over her little forty-seven-year-old son.)

"Absolutely, Joan." (Mum, patting Gran on the hand, 'cause she understood Gran was also fretting about not having an excuse to hang out at our place so much, and not having all of us to fill up her days.)

"And what about you, Nicola, dear? How are you feeling about going back to work next week, and leaving Martha at home with Will?" (Gran, fretting over her darling not-really-grandchild being left with a useless male. She liked Will, but presumed that, same as Dad, every grown-up man was incapable of looking after himself, never mind a baby.)

"Oh, I think it'll work out just dandy!" (Mum, trying to sound all cheery and positive, though at the mention of work and leaving Martha, she manically started folding and refolding one of my little sister's bibs.)

On the way home from school I'd reminded myself to pester Mum about Dad's soon-to-be-vacated room. But the woman-to-older-woman chat I'd walked in on seemed a bit too intense to interrupt, so I shoved my room-begging plans to the back of my mind and offered (in my "dependable" and "capable" way) to take hop-a-long Dog to the vet down the road instead, since no one *else* seemed to have thought to do it so far.

And now here I was, bored, and passing the time by having a staring competition with a dog with raisins for eyes.

"Dog Bird?" a vet I hadn't seen before suddenly called out from the door of the consulting room.

Urgh. . . I forgot that was the policy here – the staff always called out the pet's name and the client's surname together. It'd probably sound cute if a little old lady called Mrs Thomson took her cat Tigger in. It just sounded slightly bizarre in our case. Sure enough, the bull terrier's owner did a double take at the contents of our wicker cat box, in case a strange, new, hybrid beast was inside.

I quickly picked up Dog and kept the front of the basket turned away from the bull terrier's owner, just to keep up the mystery.

"So. . ." said the vet, patting the examining table that Dog had been on so very many times before. "Dog's an unusual name for a cat!"

For a second, I felt like telling her that it was a tradition in our family to have unusual names. I sort of felt like telling her that my name was Butterfly and my twin's name was *Bee*.

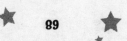

But then she started stroking Dog really warmly and I ditched the dumb name scam straightaway.

"Seemed like a good idea at the time," I said with a shrug.

"Poor Dog seems to be a bit accident-prone!" the vet continued, glancing at the list of Bird family visits on the consulting room computer screen.

"You can say that again. . ." I mumbled. Dog had already gone into overtime with her nine lives. She'd fallen out of a tree, eaten a whole ball of string, jumped on to a greenhouse glass roof that gave way under her and been run over by a pizza-delivery moped. And those were only the ones I could remember. We'd sniffled and snuffled and expected her to die umpteen times in her furry little life.

When I was about eight, and she was on death's door for whatever reason, I'd even planned out a whole funeral for her, picking a certain spot in the garden where she likes to poo, where I thought she might like to be buried. I'd decided on dandelions for the grave, and music (the theme from *Neighbours* – it always got her purring). I'd been quite taken by the idea of her funeral by the end. I remember asking my mum if there was such a thing as animal undertakers, as I quite fancied being one when I grew up. Maybe I'd suggest it as a sideline to Dad's new downstairs neighbours. . .

"So, what's happened to your poor puss this time?" asked the vet, noting that Dog couldn't put any weight on her back leg.

"My brother kicked her off a wall. With a football."

"Deliberately?" the vet asked, sort of shocked.

I was so angry with Sonny, that I almost said yes. But even *I* couldn't be that mean.

"No, not deliberately," I told the vet.

"No, not deliberately," I told Dad, ten minutes later, once I'd walked around to his work unit, a couple of minutes away from the vet surgery.

Dad hadn't got in till late last night, and was – as usual – up early and off out to work, and had missed the whole Sonny-whacked-Dog saga.

"And what's it called again? The thing that's wrong?" asked Dad, sticking his fingers through the cat basket door, so Dog could rub herself against them for comfort.

"A cruciate ligament," I said, repeating what the vet told me. "It must've got torn when she landed."

Daryl and Kemal – who worked with Dad –

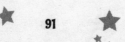

paused with big boxes in their arms and winced.

"So how long's she got to stay in the whatd'youmacallit?"

I hadn't just come round to tell tales on Sonny. The vet had prescribed a chunk of enforced bed rest for Dog, and since cats don't generally listen to good advice, we needed to get hold of a big dog cage to keep her in, till the damaged ligament healed. And as dog cages were big, heavy and expensive, I needed Dad to zoom round and get one from the pet shop in his work van.

"Eight weeks," I told him.

"Eight *weeks*?!" said Dad in surprise, as Daryl and Kemal put down their boxes and came over to coo sympathetically at poor Dog. "Can't they put a plaster cast on her leg instead?"

"Yeah, and then she could hop around the garden on tiny cat crutches!" I said, raising my eyebrows at his stupid comment.

Dad nodded. "Oh, of course. Sure – I'll shut up here early and get the cage."

Even though I could tell he was genuinely sorry for Dog, part of Dad's brain was still elsewhere: all the while, his fingers were tap-tap-tapping along to some track that was blasting from the radio playing in the background.

"Well—"

The rest of my sentence was going to be "I'll see you back at the house", but Dad jumped in with something else before I could leave.

"Sonny was a bit weird this morning. . . Do you think it might be because he hurt Dog?" Dad asked, as Daryl and Kemal ambled back to their work.

"You saw Sonny this morning?" I asked, wondering what my brother was doing up at the crack of dawn, i.e. the time Dad had to set off to open up for the early-bird stream of customers who seemed in desperate need of the paper plates, napkins, plastic cups and cutlery he stocked.

"Yeah – he was hovering around in the kitchen when I was leaving. He didn't mention Dog, though. But maybe he was feeling guilty, and just checking on her or something?"

"Maybe. . ." I muttered, at first thinking that *could* be a reason, but then remembering that Sonny had been in a strange sort of mood even *before* he splatted Dog with the football. "It's funny, but when he came in from school yesterday—"

"Hold it!" said Dad, his hand aloft and his eyes alight. Some dramatic thought had entered his head, diverting him from the worried-about-Sonny conversation we'd just been having.

Surely it was something important.

Ha.

"*. . .and today's competition IS a bit of a belter, though I say so myself!!*" the DJ on the radio was gabbling smugly.

"Ace!" Dad muttered, obviously listening intently.

Fantastic. So I already knew that Dad was mad on music, and mad on listening to the radio all day at work, and also mad on music-related phone-in competitions on the radio. I just didn't realize he was *so* mad on them that they were more important than an idiot like Sonny, and whatever might be bothering him.

"See you," I said grumpily, grabbing hold of Dog's basket and turning to go.

"Oh, hey," said Dad, breaking his concentration to say one more thing to me. "Is Will OK?"

"Will?" I frowned. "I guess so. Why?"

As far as I knew, Will was *more* than OK; he was ecstatic. Ecstatic that Dad was moving out – but I wasn't about to say that, of course.

"Well, when I went to the loo last night, I heard a noise in the kitchen and came downstairs. And there was Will, squashing things."

"Squashing *what* things?" I frowned at Dad. Bugs? Whoopee cushions?

"Bananas. And stuff that was maybe swede."

Duh. OK, so squashed bananas and stuff that was maybe swede might not be the sort of thing any of us would drool over, but it was *exactly* the sort of thing six-month-old babies adored. Mum made that kind of gloop all the time for Martha.

"It's no big deal," I said with a shrug. "Will must've just been getting some baby food practice in."

"I suppose," said Dad, nodding his head in time to the track that had just come on the radio in the background. "It just seemed weird, since it was 2.30 a.m."

Huh? I knew Will was a bit of a perfectionist, but food preparation in the middle of the night seemed ever so slightly insane.

"What did he say?" I asked.

"Said he'd popped down for a glass of water and got sidetracked," said Dad vaguely, as if he wasn't sure if that sounded totally reasonable or not.

Ha. It was about as reasonable as cheese-flavoured chocolate.

"And then I was out in the van delivering some supplies this morning," Dad wittered on, before I got the chance to actually say anything. "I saw

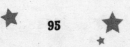

him on his way to the tube station and . . . and he was biting his nails."

Nail-biting? Will, the secretly obsessive-compulsive tidier and self-proclaimed "everything's cool" guy *always* had perfectly short, perfectly neat nails. When Will moved in, a whole shelf in the bathroom was soon cluttered up with what men's magazines call "grooming" products (which sounds suspiciously like something to do with horses to me).

I mean, Will just wasn't the nail-biting type. I bet he even pushed back his cuticles (though I didn't really know what they were – I just read about them in the beauty pages of Mum's mags). Even my dippy dad knew that nail-biting was way out of character for Mum's boyfriend.

"Don't know what *that's* all about." I shrugged, making a mental note to nosey at Will's fingernails over tea tonight. And listen out for the sound of middle-of-the-night baby recipes.

Will and Sonny, Sonny and Will.

So what exactly was going on with two of the three useless males in my family?

Who knew.

I didn't bother to talk it over any more with Dad, as this particular useless male had gone back to listening to his radio phone-in competition. . .

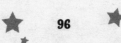

Itchy thinking

It was like magic.

Me and Sonny had been trying to help Dad pack for an hour now, and his room looked fuller than ever.

I think a bad witch must have cast a big mess spell on the place while we weren't looking. Or maybe it was just 'cause every time any of us pulled open a drawer or took stuff off a shelf, Dad started gazing lovingly at the CDs, or magazines, or concert programmes or whatever it was we'd dragged out.

"Look at this!" he said, holding up a small, insignificant-looking ticket. "Talking Heads, 1977. What a show – it blew me away!"

It had been the same with a programme for a Blondie gig ("Debbie Harry – wow! I mean, *wow!*"), a complete set of Q magazines from 1986–2007 ("The bible of music!!") and an album that had fallen down the side of the bed.

"Listen to this!" said Dad, flipping open the dusty CD case.

I didn't look round. If I'd looked round every time Dad had got excited about something over the last hour, I'd've ended up with a crick in my neck, and Dad wouldn't have had at least *one* suitcase full of neatly packed clothes. By me, of course.

Sonny didn't look up either. He'd stopped trying to help in the face of the total shambles and gone to get his guitar instead. He'd been quietly strumming along to whatever track Dad had been blasting, and it was pretty nice actually.

Yes, I'd used the word "nice" in the same sentence as my brother. Freaky, huh? I still hadn't figured out what was up with him this week, but during the last three days – ever since the Dog-splatting incident – Sonny had been unusually quiet. It was a bit odd. More than a bit odd. Very oddly odd. But I was enjoying the peace and quiet too much to give myself brain-strain trying to figure it out.

"Watch out – *this* is going to bring back memories!!" Dad called out in a sing-song, jovial warning as he walked over to the CD player.

I gave in and flopped down on to the floor to

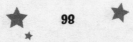

watch him, thinking how much I was going to miss my dad and his uselessness and enthusiasm.

It was just a shame he wasn't more enthusiastic about packing: after all, he was supposed to be shifting everything tomorrow morning, but at this rate, he'd still be trundling back and forth for bits and pieces for the next few weeks.

And until the clutter was finally gone, and the pizza boxes and stray socks and dustballs were cleared away, there was no way I could even *begin* to imagine myself in here. Not that I'd got round to bringing up the subject with Mum yet, anyway; between reassuring Gran, swotting up for work next week, and stressing over leaving Martha, Mum had been so preoccupied that there'd never been a right time to talk to her on her own yet.

"PARA-PAA-PAA-PARA-PA-PAH-PAHHH!!"

Hey – the opening bars of "Chicken Payback" by The Bees! Both Sonny and me automatically broke into smiles as wide as Dad's. This song was as stupid as it was fantastic and as groovy as it was nuts. The words were ditzy nonsense, all about chickens and monkeys and pigs. It was the one track that was guaranteed to get us all up and dancing – even Mum – whenever it got played, so Dad liked to play it a *lot*, back when he lived in the main house (i.e. pre-split, and pre-Will and Martha).

"Remember how we used to make up silly dances to this?" asked Dad, holding a hand out to me and pulling me up off the floor. Sonny, pinned to the tan leather chair by his guitar, looked on, laughing.

"Rock'n'roll!" I called out, as Dad spun me under his arm.

"Salsa!" ordered Dad, trying and failing to zig-zag me back and forth (that's the one he used to do with Mum).

"Pogo!!" I giggled, bouncing up and down on the spot, as Dad thumped opposite me, his T-shirt flapping to reveal his sprawling tum.

"Opera style!" Dad shouted next, launching into a booming yell of "*Do the Chicken Payback!*" which I matched with a trilling falsetto.

"Boy-band style!!" Dad ordered, his eyes wide as he remembered this particular silliness.

Even though it had been ages, I jumped right beside him, immediately launching into one of those corny, cheesy synchronized dance steps that only boy bands do.

"Come on!" Dad urged Sonny, waving at him to join us. It was only properly funny when there was enough of us doing it to look like a boy band.

And, OK, Mum wasn't here to make it four, but three could just about work.

"Nah. . ." said Sonny, his face suddenly clouding over. He stood up, taking his guitar, and left, just like that.

"Maybe I should go after him," muttered Dad, walking over to press pause on the CD player. "See what's wrong. . ."

"I don't know for sure, but I think maybe he just needs time to get used to all this," I suggested, waving my hand around the room to refer to Dad leaving (and not his mess, of course).

"Me going?" said Dad, scratching his head.

Duh. Hadn't he thought we might miss him? Didn't I say (like, a *hundred* times) that he was useless?

"Well, yeah," I said with a shrug – and then *another* thought occurred to me. "Y'know, maybe that track just reminded him of you and Mum and us all together or something."

"Yeah?" said Dad, scratching his chin this time. All this deep thinking seemed to be making him itchy. "I'll go talk to your brother. . ."

I'm not too sentimental – not like Sonny – but once Dad left, I kind of didn't want to be on my own in his room, with all his stuff strewn around. It gave me this little tinge of sadness, like some

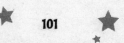

tiny misery gremlin had pinched me. So I headed on downstairs, thinking I'd quite like to flop on the sofa beside Mum and cuddle Clyde, or maybe check in on poor Dog, who was in her mini-prison (the giant cage Dad had picked up) wearing a plastic lampshade-style collar to keep her from biting at her tight leg bandage. We'd set the cage up by the TV and were leaving it on all day to keep her company, and she seemed to be quite enjoying the daytime soaps, cookery and home decor shows on there.

". . .so come on, let's see it!" I heard Mum say, as I reached the bottom of the stairs.

She must be talking to Will. I checked my watch – it wasn't very late; I hadn't expected him to be home so soon. It's not like I knew too much about leaving dos, but I thought they involved lots of people from your work dragging you to the pub to drink too much beer, as a way of saying bye. Will's leaving do seemed to have finished at a fairly sensible time. Or maybe he was just tired after bizarre late-night cooking sessions.

"Hi!" I said, wandering into the living room. "What's that?"

Mum was holding something up against Will. Grinning, he turned around for me to see.

"My leaving present," he said sheepishly.

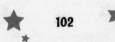

"'*Danger – Dad in charge*!!'" I read the logo on the red T-shirt out loud. "You aren't *actually* going to go out wearing that, are you?"

Jokey T-shirts always make me cringe. It's like the people wearing them are trying to say, "Me? I'm *so* funny!!", when they plainly aren't. Maybe I should get one for that not-funny young guy who was going to be Dad's new neighbour. . .

"I don't think so," laughed Will, who might use the word "cool" too much for his own good, but at least had decent taste in clothes.

"So what did everyone have to say to you?" Mum asked, keen for all the gossip from Will's night out.

Since I knew exactly *none* of Will's teacher buddies, my mind kind of glazed over the chat at this point. Instead, I picked up a big card – a sorry-you're-leaving card, I supposed – that Will had dumped on the back of the sofa, along with his jacket.

The front of it was pretty funny – someone had done a caricature of Will in his PE tracksuit, racing down a running track and pushing a pram with a startled-looking baby peering out of it. Inside the card was a scrawl of messages, all higgledy-piggledy, in shades of black, blue and red biro.

They were all different, but all along the same lines: a jokey remark about Will's new job ("From circuit training to potty training, you're the man for the job!") followed by some gushy comment ("Going to miss you, big guy!") and signed off with some squiggle of a name (with kisses after, if it was from a female – hopefully).

I was just about to shut the card and go get some treat or other from the fridge for Dog, when my eyes settled on one message down in the left-hand corner. Yes, it was pretty much a carbon copy of the others, except that after "Leah xxx" came "PS If you need me, just call. . ."

Er, who was Leah, and why would Will need her, exactly?

And then it dawned on me: on Tuesday evening, in the blur of taking care of Dog, I'd semi-forgotten that comment Dad had made about Will looking nervous on the way to work. I'd completely forgotten to spy on Will up close.

"Uh, fancy a tea or something?" I said, mooching over towards Mum and Will.

"Yes, please, darling!" said Mum, slightly startled at my daughterly thoughtfulness.

"Yeah, that'd be cool, Sadie!" said Will, his arm resting along the back of the sofa.

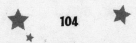

And yes, his normally neat nails were bitten right down.

"If you need me, just call . . . if you need me, just call . . . if you need me, just call. . ."

The words looped around my brain as I walked in a puzzled daze towards the kitchen. . .

Strangely strange

Next time you see a white workmen's van, check out the guys inside (it's always guys).

There'll be three of them (big white workmen's vans are wide enough to sit three in the cab). One will be driving, one will be reading the newspaper, and one will have his feet up on the dashboard. It's like some unwritten law that *that's* how you've got to be positioned.

In our white van today, Will was flicking through a newspaper, Dad was driving, and I (breaking the white van/guys-only rule!) was the one with my feet on the dashboard.

"Sadie, why do you always wear your trainers like that?" asked Dad.

"I dunno," I answered, tapping together the toes of my heels-tucked-in Converse All-Stars. No, I hadn't learned my lesson after trying to run in them this time last week. And when I was lying face down, practically tasting pavement, little did

I expect that in seven short days I'd be helping my dad move house. (Thoughts running through my head at that particular point were more along the lines of "could I *be* any more embarrassed?" and, "are my kneecaps broken?").

"I think it looks cool."

No prizes for guessing that was Will talking. I'd have appreciated his comment more if I wasn't feeling so strangely strange about him just now. I just couldn't figure out what to make of the bizarre middle-of-the-night baby food fest, the bitten nails and the scribbled message I'd seen in his leaving card last night. I'd've been tempted to talk to Dad about it, but this morning was just a flurry of last-minute removals, with Mum and Gran on packing duty, while me, Will and Dad stacked stuff in the back of the van. Note the absence of Sonny: he'd had to go to stage school for a rehearsal or an audition or some other excuse that conveniently got him out of helping with the hard work.

And anyway, talking to your mum's ex (Dad) about her new bloke (Will) was all a bit icky and awkward and weird somehow.

Still, as far as the Will thing went, maybe I couldn't make sense of it, but I could always drop a casual remark in the conversation, and see where it got me, couldn't I?

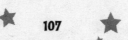

"Hey! They're looking worse than *mine*!" I said, holding my hand up against one of Will's. Dad coughed.

"Um, d'you think so?" said Will, letting go of one side of the paper as he held his hand up to compare bitten nails. "Actually I think *yours* look worse. At least *I* don't have chipped orange nail varnish!"

Ooh, he did well there. Sounded slightly caught out at the beginning of the sentence, and then slid into a bit of teasing at my expense.

Ha – he didn't get out of it that easily, though!

"I'll lend you some of my orange nail varnish if you want! But since when did you start biting your nails?" I asked Will, feeling Dad wriggle uncomfortably next to me in the driving seat.

"Well . . . this week, I guess. I hadn't even realized I was doing it. But it's been a madly busy time, trying to get everything sorted at work before I left."

OK, so that was an excuse. A pretty *lame* one, though. I mean, what does a PE teacher have to get madly busy sorting out? It's not like there would be a mountain of paperwork. Had he been running himself ragged stacking up the footballs neatly? Or piling up the beanbags in colour-coded mounds?!

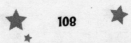

Had fretting over footballs and beanbags turned him into an insomniac who blended in the night when he couldn't sleep?

Even if the baby food thing and the bitten nails issues were *possibly* answered, it didn't solve the riddle of the cryptic card message. But I couldn't think of anything flippant to say to get him talking about *that*. . .

"Here we are!" said Dad, pulling up outside the undertaker's. There was a ladder in front of the shop. (Can you call an undertaker's a shop? "Let's see . . . could I have one of your walnut caskets and, oooh, two of those lovely funeral wreaths, please?")

I ducked my head down for a better look out of the windscreen as Dad parked, and saw an old bloke in overalls painstakingly adding a painted golden "s" to the end of the "McConnell & Son" sign.

Good grief, I thought, as reality kicked in again. *Is this really where Dad wants to call home? Is this really where I'll be coming to hang out with him? How depressing*. . .

"Right, let's get you moved in, then, Max!" said Will, a bit too cheerfully, slapping his hands together before he opened the van door.

Luckily, Dad didn't seem to detect any signs of

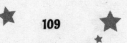

total relief on Will's part, and just gratefully accepted the help. This didn't stop me quietly resenting how Sonny had sloped off to his precious stage school, leaving me to schlep armloads of albums and general Dad-clutter.

"Hey, what did Sonny say last night, when you went after him?" I asked Dad, who came puffing in behind me. I'd kind of let Sonny's "Chicken Payback" huff slip to the back of my mind, what with the Will thing and the hectic-ness of this morning.

"Uh . . . he didn't say much, really," said Dad, thunking his box down heavily and then wincing at the tinkling, breaking sort of sound from inside. "He just said he was really tired, that's all. There's been lots going on at school apparently, and he's been doing extra stuff at lunchtimes – some new project with that new teacher he mentioned. Benny or someone."

"Was that it?" I asked, frowning. Typical. There I was feeling slightly (only *slightly*, mind) sorry for Sonny, thinking he was getting upset about Dad moving out, yadda, yadda, yadda. But all the time he was just mumphing over extra work at school. Maybe this Benny he'd been raving about last week was turning out to be a pain – maybe he was bursting Sonny's show-biz bubble and telling him that he wasn't about to be the next Daniel Radcliffe or whoever.

"Hey, cool place, Max!" said Will, coming into the room behind us. "So . . . what're you going to do about furniture?"

"Furniture?" said Dad, blinking at Will as if he'd never heard the word before in all his experience of the English language.

"Dad – you have *thought* about furniture, haven't you?" I asked him, instantly realizing that the answer, of course, was no. Had he really expected to furnish the place with the contents of his BP? Mind you, he probably thought that a TV, a minifridge, a bed, a CD player, a tan leather chair and a filing cabinet for your underwear was pretty much perfect.

I could tell that once we were finished here, I'd have to take him by the hand and drag him and his credit card round IKEA all afternoon. . .

"Um, sorry to disturb you. . ." A voice drifted through from the open front door, accompanied by a nervous knock.

"Come on in!" said Dad, as his teenage neighbour – Mr Not-Funny – hovered self-consciously in the hallway. What was his name again? Something Celtic-sounding . . . Calum or Conor. No – I remembered, Cormac.

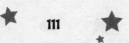

111

Anyway, Cormac looked somehow weirder than the last time I'd seen him. It was 'cause of the way he was dressed; last weekend he'd been in standard jeans and a T-shirt, but today he was wearing a black suit, for goodness' sake, and a black tie. It was the hair too; that shock of vivid ginger was even more shocking against funereal black. What was he in that ultra-straight get-up for? I felt like asking if someone had *died*.

"Um, is that your van outside?" he asked us tentatively.

"Yep, it's mine!" Dad beamed.

"Well, my father sent me up to ask if you'd mind moving it – it's just that we've got a hearse arriving in a couple of minutes and it needs to park right outside. . ."

Yeah, Dad, I thought, as I clocked how speechless he was for a second. *Welcome to your new world!*

And then I stopped silently sniggering at Dad and felt a bit speechless myself.

It suddenly sunk in.

Cormac was dressed that way, 'cause someone really *had* died.

"Of course!" Dad roused himself, rifling in his pockets for his keys.

"You're the 's', aren't you?" I heard myself ask

112

Cormac out loud.

"Sorry?" muttered Cormac, looking flushed and confused.

Oh, yes, it had just dawned on me that this wannabe stand-up comedian must've just joined the family firm. He had to be the "s" on the McConnell & Son(s) sign.

My dad didn't just have an undertaker's below him, he had a trainee undertaker living above him.

It would be like living in a gloom sandwich.

Nice.

Not. . .

The horribly loud brain whisper

"Bet *that* shook the careers advisor at his school!" giggled Hannah.

"Yeah! They probably dread people coming to see them and saying they want to be pop stars or models or premier league footballers or something—"

"And then along comes – what's his name again?"

"Cormac."

"Right, this Cormac comes along and says, 'I'd like to be a funeral director, please!' Can you imagine their *face*!!"

Me and Hannah were lolling on a mound of cushions on the floor of her bedroom, supposedly watching some Saturday night celebrity singing competition on her telly, but instead we'd just been yakking and catching up. Hannah was pretty impressed with my week's events; compared to a dad moving out, a brother acting weird, a splatted cat, some Will mystery and a teenage boy who was a part-time un-comedian and a full-time undertaker, all she had to talk about was how her brother Harry had filled her vinyl pencil case with custard, which hadn't been much fun to discover at the start of Wednesday's French test. (What's French for "gloop"?)

"I know; I just don't get it. What young guy would want a job like that?" I said, flopping my head back on to the squashy cushions. "I mean, just 'cause the rest of your family do something, it doesn't mean *you* have to."

"What, you mean you *don't* want a career in the paper plate and plastic spoon industry, Sadie?" said Hannah, clasping her hands to her face in mock surprise.

"Shut up!" I laughed, grabbing a floppy cushion and aiming it at her head.

Knock-knock!!

"Ignore it! It's just Harry," Hannah mumbled, her giggles melting away at the sound of tapping on her bedroom door.

"At least he knocks. . ." I said, thinking of Sonny walking in on me in my undies.

"Yeah, he knocks, then runs away. Or knocks, and then you find a piece of string stretched over

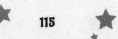

the doorway for you to trip over. He's been doing stuff like this all week. It's *soooo* irritating."

"Can't you say something to your parents?" I asked, without thinking.

Hannah shot me a "Yeah, *that'll* be right!" look. Her mum and dad were totally besotted with their little prince (bit like mine with Sonny), and chalked up all his horrid little pranks as charming high spirits. *Ha*.

Knock-knock!!

"Honestly, he'll get bored and go. It's the best way," sighed Hannah. "So what do you think is going on with your mum's boyfriend? Do you maybe think Will's having a mad, passionate affair with this woman at his school?"

She was joking.

Obviously.

So I joked back, saying that this Leah person who'd signed the card must have had a thing for men in nylon tracksuits.

Then the joking got more silly and surreal, but I couldn't remember any of it because despite the fact that I was laughing and joining in, my brain was muttering "*Is* Will seeing someone else?" over and over again in a horribly loud whisper.

"Um, just going to the loo," I said at one point in the joking.

I genuinely needed to go, but I also needed a break from the bizarre turn this conversation had taken. I needed to shake stupid thoughts out of my head and get real.

"Will's great, Mum and him are great, it's all rubbish. . ." I murmured to myself, as I sat down on the reassuringly cool toilet seat.

I felt my shoulders *just* start to relax when another, more unpleasant sensation caught me by surprise. It was warm, it was wet, and it was coursing down the back of my legs.

"Oh!!" I gasped, louder than I realized, as I jumped up.

"Hee, hee!" came the sound of "high spirited" giggling from outside the bathroom door.

I glanced back round at the toilet, and saw what I hadn't spotted before – cling film stretched across the top of the bowl. I'd fallen for the oldest, naffest trick in the book.

I wanted to fling open the bathroom door, grab Harry, turn him upside down and use his stupid head as a mop.

Instead, I grabbed frantically at the toilet roll to do the necessary floor-drying, and then realized there was hardly any loo paper left. In a panic, I gazed around. . . I couldn't use the turquoise hand towel; you could hardly flush *that* down the toilet after. And then – yay – I spotted a whole new loo roll up on top of the bathroom cabinet.

To reach it, I stepped on to the edge of the bath, and stretched up.

Pity the soles of my shoes were now wet, and I slipped.

Pity I grabbed the shower curtain to try and stop myself from falling.

Pity I ended up lying on my back, jeans undone, in a puddle of my own wee, semi-covered with a shower curtain and dismantled rail, and a hand twisted under my back. A hand that was now throbbing like crazy.

Pity I couldn't have just broken my neck in the fall and *died*, and saved myself a whole mountain of embarrassment.

I'd cheerfully strangle Harry next time I saw him – if my hand wasn't quite possibly broken. . .

Crump lava

"Did you know that if you laid a million babies end-to-end, they would stretch all the way from Acapulco in Mexico to Pyongyang in North Korea?" I said, pretending to read from a book that was actually upside down.

Martha gazed up at me from her buggy.

"And here's an interesting fact: the youngest baby to walk was only *three* months old. Her parents entered her for her first five-kilometre Fun Run when she was only two!"

Martha blinked.

"And did you know that if you feed babies peas too young, they stay light green *for ever*?"

Martha pulled a funny face. I think she might have been filling her nappy. . .

Y'know, playing "Boo!" a hundred times in a row gets a bit dull, so it's fun telling lies to babies. It's all very innocent, 'cause they haven't a clue

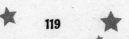

what you're saying so you're not exactly messing with their tiny minds.

I guess today's lies were a form of boredom-busting, though. I mean, I love, love, *loved* Martha, but tiny babies don't exactly *do* much, and sometimes you need to while away the time while they're snoozing, or just sitting there, filling their nappies or whatever.

So first there were the lies, and then there were the inappropriate books.

"How about this one!" I said, reaching across to the nearest bookshop shelf and randomly lifting a copy of something called *The First Emperor: Caesar Augustus and the Triumph of Rome*, and holding it out for my sis to peruse. "Think you'll find it very, *very* educational!"

Martha cooed and reached out ten fat fingers to give the book a hug and quite possibly a suck.

"No, actually – think you'll like *this* one better!"

I plonked the first book back and made a grab for a heavy hardback called *Roget's Thesaurus of English Words and Phrases*.

Yeowwww!!

I had managed to forget for a second that I was suffering from a practical-joke injury, but I remembered pretty quickly once the pain of lifting something I shouldn't have shot *right* up my hand.

It wasn't broken, by the way.

I guess that should've been a relief, but my shame was so huge that sixteen hours after my flop on the bathroom floor of Hannah's house and I was *still* blushing to the roots of my dark hair.

During those first couple of seconds as I lay in my shocked state, I'd feebly hoped I might somehow manage to scramble myself up, hobble to Hannah's room and get her to help me out with the minimum of fuss. Yeah, *right*. I'd made such a thump on the bathroom floor that Hannah's parents were outside the door like a shot, hammering and calling out, and obviously confused about what toilet-related disaster had just happened.

Even now, I'm going to blur out the mortifying details (like opening the bathroom door on my knees, struggling to pull my wet jeans up with my one good hand, a huddle of faces staring at me . . . urgh). Still the *one* good thing – according to Hannah's text this morning – was that it had finally dawned on her parents that Harry's funny little obsession with practical jokes was in no way endearing *or* remotely funny. Apparently, they were going to get Harry to apologize to me, next time I came round.

Ha – they were fools if they thought me and my embarrassment would be back round their house any time this century. . .

"Aaah-eeee!!" gurgled Martha happily.

"Exactly!" I nodded down into the buggy.

I hadn't a clue what she was on about. Living with babies is a bit like having someone from a different country or a different *planet* living with you. They speak another language.

So apart from telling my little sister lies, showing her inappropriate books and wishing I could find a Baby Gurgling–English translation dictionary on the shelves here, what exactly was I doing in Waterstone's, Islington Green, on a Sunday morning?

Well, just passing the time, half-heartedly checking out some books I needed for school while on babysitting duties.

At first, me and Martha had quite happily wandered down Upper Street, till I got paranoid that people were staring at me, thinking I was an exceptionally young teenage mum.

Actually, they were probably more likely to have been glancing at the gleaming white bandage on my hand (lucky Hannah's mum is a nurse).

Course, maybe they were staring at me because

I looked like an exceptionally young teenage mum who'd been beaten up by her baby's father. . .

Then again, maybe no one was really staring at me at all, and I was just being paranoid. But anyway, I'd decided to give my paranoid self a break and duck into the nearest store to browse, and that store happened to be Waterstone's.

Anyway, the reason I was babysitting was that back home, Mum was in a light frenzy, getting all geared up to start back at work tomorrow. And Will? Will was doing a mega-shop at the supermarket, in preparation for the next five days of Daddy duty (he'd be buying nappies etc. in bulk – Will buys *everything* in bulk, like he's trying to show everyone how capable he is as a grown-up, step-family man, or like he's expecting a *siege* to happen any day).

So I got saddled with looking after Martha. Which of course I didn't really mind, but I say "saddled" 'cause somehow it was always *me* who got the "can you take care of Martha for a bit?" plea, and never Sonny. Oh, *no* – Sonny's time was always too precious, what with rehearsing for some play or practising his jazz hands or whatever. (This translates as: Sonny = special; Sadie = idle, unremarkable and twiddling her thumbs.)

"Ah-hunggggg. . .."

Uh-oh. For inexplicable small baby reasons, Martha had switched from happy goo-goo-ing to an on-the-verge-of-crying whine.

"Here! Here, Martha! Look at the cute bunny!" I held up my bandaged-together, staved fingers, and tried to make the "bunny" dance in an entertaining manner.

Martha was having none of it.

"Ah-huungggg, ah-hunnnnggg, ah—"

OK, sobs were three seconds away. I had to act fast: I scrabbled around in my bag and found a pen. I scribbled a quick and – sadly – slightly *scary* looking rabbit's face on my bandage.

"Waaaahhhhhhhh! Waaaahhhhhhh!! Hic, hic, waaaaaahhhhh!"

"Shush, honey!" I said in my softest, most comforting voice, which probably came out as more tense and tetchy, since we were in a public place.

"Waaaahhhhhhhh! Waaaahhhhhhhh!!"

"Sadie? What's up?"

Will?

What was Will doing in this bookshop? Wasn't he meant to be buying up half of Sainsbury's stock of baby wipes right now?

"I *thought* I heard Martha!" said Will, bending

down to the small pair of arms that were suddenly stretching up to him. "I didn't know you, um, girls were going to be here!"

Sheepish: it's a stupid word. I mean, Will didn't *look* like a sheep; he just looked like he'd been caught doing something he shouldn't have been doing. Maybe it's a well-kept farmers' secret that sheep are deeply shady characters, and that's where the word comes from. . .

"Looking for books for school," I said, sort of flatly, not adding "and what are YOU doing here?", but wanting to.

"Yeah? Cool!" said Will, pushing his hair back off his face before lifting Martha out of the buggy for a comforting cuddle. "I was just. . . having a quick look round for a new book to read, before I, uh, headed off to the supermarket. Hey, since Martha's a bit upset, why don't I take her with *me*?"

"Cool," I replied, using Will-speak, and feeling anything but cool.

I mean, it was lovely to see how much Martha loved her daddy (just look at her snuggling into him).

But, but, but.

But something was bugging me and I couldn't figure out what. . .

*

125

I'd figured it out.

It was something – *two* somethings – Will had done back in the bookshop, around the same time he'd said, "Sadie?", and "I *thought* I heard Martha!".

And weird situation or not, I wanted to talk to Dad about it. So now that I was baby-free, I'd found myself on the pavement outside McConnell & Sons, buzzing Dad's buzzer and thundering up the stairs to his flat.

"Hey, Sadie!" said Dad. "Wasn't expecting to see you today!"

It had been exactly seventeen hours now since my absolute shame in Hannah's bathroom. And it had been twenty hours since I last saw Dad, as I helped him unload a bundle of IKEA flatpack furniture from his van. I hadn't stayed around for the assembling and swearing bit. . .

"Hi, Dad," I said, noticing the hall *still* had furniture flatpacks stacked against the wall. By the looks of it, Dad hadn't exactly dived headfirst into a whirl of DIY yet.

"Come on in!" He ushered me in warmly. "It's great; I've got the TV and DVD rigged up to come out of the speakers, so it sounds awesome! And *wait* till you see the new toy I went out and bought myself this morning!"

Useless. He'd sorted out the entertainment in his new BP, but hadn't got a *bed*. (Glancing through to the bedroom, I could see the frame still boxed up, and the new double mattress enveloped in its vast plastic bag.)

"Where did you sleep last night?" I asked Dad, frowning.

"In there for now, on my old single bed from the garage," said Dad, pointing to the boxroom next to the bathroom, which I'd only just discovered yesterday afternoon, when I nipped to the loo and took a wrong turn. Dad had been very enthusiastic about it, saying that me or Sonny could stay over any time we wanted.

Ahem.

Much as me and Sonny both loved our dad, I couldn't see why either of us would want to stay in a glorified cupboard above an undertaker's, when our own comfy bedrooms were five minutes' walk away. Especially when my bedroom might soon be the very *excellent* room above the garage. . .

"Never mind about that!" said Dad, impatient to show me what he'd been playing with. "Come and check this out!"

I think I was supposed to marvel at the new, huge wide-screen TV he had set up, or maybe the

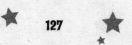

sound blasting out of the speakers now perched on packing boxes.

But mostly I was marvelling at how comfy and at home Sonny and Cormac looked.

"Uh, hi!"

That was Cormac. He was sitting – in normal clothes and not the funeral suit, thankfully – on one of a pair of folding chairs Dad had bought to go with a folding table yesterday. Dad must've been sitting on the other one, 'cause Sonny had sprawled himself all over the tan leather armchair.

There was a half-eaten pizza in a box on the floor between them, and an open can of Coke by each chair.

"I bumped into Cormac and his big brother on the stairs last night, and we got chatting about various comedians," said Dad, by way of some sort of explanation that didn't really make any sense to me.

I hadn't seen the rest of Cormac's family yet. Wasn't in a mad rush to, to be honest. Could you imagine them starring in that card game Happy Families? "Can I swap you a Mrs Bun the Baker's Wife for Master Dead the Undertaker's Son?"

"Ah, but let me get you a drink first, Sadie,"

mumbled Dad, coming over all hospitable as he went through to the kitchen, where his minifridge would probably still be plonked on the draining board where it got "temporarily" placed yesterday.

"Hey, have you seen this bloke, Sadie? It's Cormac's DVD. This guy's *so* funny!!" said Sonny, pointing at the giant TV, where a comedian was strolling around a stage, drily telling jokes.

"No," I replied, standing stony still, with a face to match.

Of *course* I knew who it was; it was Dylan Moran. He was this Irish guy whose accent always reminded me of Gran's.

"He's called Dylan Moran – he's really, really good!" Cormac tried explaining to me, his eyes flicking down for a second to my bandaged hand.

Ooh, I could feel a grumpy mood wash right over me. I was grumpy with Dad for acting like a big kid and not sorting out his new flat. I was grumpy with Sonny for somehow sloping off and hanging out here, while I'd been left to baby-sit. I was grumpy with Cormac, for looking so at home in my dad's living room. I was grumpy with Will for a) weirdly hiding a book behind his back when he came over to us in Waterstone's, b) then stuffing it hurriedly on a shelf, and c) nodding a "bye" at someone I couldn't see as he was talking to us. And I was grumpy because my stupid hand hurt like *mad*.

I was like a simmering volcano of grumpiness, and no matter how much I tried to keep a lid on it, some grump lava was bound to spray.

"No dead people to look after today?" I said, all mock brightly to Cormac.

"Uh, no. . ." he replied, squirming about in his seat a bit.

"Tell me," I continued, breezily and brusquely, "since you're a comedian, do you make jokes about the bodies that come in?"

Cormac stopped fidgeting and instead flushed bright red. I took it for an admission of mega-guilt.

"I'd *never* make jokes about someone that's just died," said Cormac hotly. "Specially not when you've just been dealing with a family that's in tears!"

Oh. Maybe that was more a red flush of *anger*.

"Just ignore her," Sonny drawled at Cormac, an annoying grin on his face. "She gets like this with me too!"

I shot my brother my most withering look.

My brother casually ignored it, which he knew would annoy me to the *max*.

"Hey, Sadie!" He grinned his lop-sided grin at

130

me. "Why don't you tell Cormac the really funny story of what happened to your hand?"

"Get lost!" I snapped at Sonny. I *knew* he'd been listening in when I was moaning to Mum about Harry and my hand last night.

"Dad! Sadie said. . ."

"DAD!" I shouted over the top of Sonny's whine. "I'VE GOT TO GO. CATCH YOU LATER."

I turned and stomped out of the flat, bumping against the wall in my hurry and ending up with a smudge of white chalk that once said "BEWARE" on my shoulder.

Muddle is such a pathetic little word, but that's what I suddenly felt like: in a total muddle, as I stomp-stomped down the stairs and yanked open the heavy front door on to the street.

The trouble was, I didn't know whether to growl or cry.

So I did both at once, which was a mad, startling kind of sound.

"RAAARRRGGHHH!-a-*hic*!!"

"Ooooh, my *good*ness!"

"Yelp!!"

Oops, I'd just managed to make a little old man and his elderly Yorkshire terrier nearly keel over in shock.

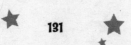

"Sorry!" I said, hoping they were all right.

I didn't really fancy running upstairs and telling Cormac I'd got him a couple of new clients.

Never mind asking him if his company happened to do very, *very* tiny dog-sized coffins. . .

I'd had better Monday afternoons

Nobody died.

Well, obviously someone, *somewhere* died, and pretty regularly, or firms like McConnell & Sons would be switching to different careers, like candyfloss salesmen or cat-sitters or something more cuddly and cheerful maybe.

I just mean I didn't frighten any unsuspecting passers-by and their pets to death yesterday after all. (I just got a major "tsking" as the old guy and his dog went on their way.)

And now it was Monday, and I'd had a day of explaining (OK, *lying*) to everyone except Letitia at school about why I had a bandage on my hand ("tripped over my rabbit"), and why I'd drawn an evil rabbit on it ("in honour of Clyde").

"*You* don't think it's that evil, do you?" I asked Clyde, kneeling down beside him as soon as I walked into the house and saw him hovering in the hall, like a faithful hound.

I held up my hand. Clyde bared his teeth, lowered his ears and hopped off into the living room.

Oh.

You know those shots you get in films, where the camera slowly pans from a character's shocked face to the cause of the shock?

Imagine that now: a camera panning down from *my* shocked face, following a lolloping Clyde along the hallway and into . . . well, a scene of total devastation, where our nice ordered living room used to be.

"Prrrp!"

I couldn't see Dog, thanks to a lemon baby blanket and a pile of what might have been washing draped all over the silver bars of her sickbay cage.

And it looked like a whole packet of Pampers had been opened, semi-stuck in a nappy shape and then strewn across the floor.

Meanwhile, the rug in the middle of the floor, plus half of the sofa, was white, as if a container of talc had exploded over it. Not that you could see much of the sofa or the carpets, thanks to the scattering of soft toys and discarded baby clothes everywhere.

It was like a bunch of teddies and dribbled-on

sleep-suits had been stuffed into a blender in the middle of the floor, only someone had switched it on without sticking the lid on top.

In the middle of all this chaos was the prone figure of Will, with Martha asleep on top of him.

"Will?" I said, wondering if my stepdad had disturbed a pack of vandals who'd broken in, and been struck down by a baby rattle to the head or something.

"Yeah-huh?!" Will replied in a fug of confusion, sitting up straight, clutching on to the still-snoozling Martha.

"What happened?" I asked, staring around me.

"Well, yeah, quite a state, isn't it?" He laughed, pulling himself into normal Will-assuredness with impressive speed. "I turned my back for two minutes to get a bottle for her from the kitchen, and when I came back, she'd done all *this*!!"

"*All* of it?" I said, gazing at my sister, who looked extra weeny small at this very moment.

"Unbelievable, isn't it?" Will answered, shaking his head wryly.

"You can say *that* again," I mumbled, bending down to start scooping up stray giraffes and size-titchy socks.

"Actually, can you take Martha for a minute? I just want to nip upstairs to check my emails. . ."

★ **135** ★

"OK." I shrugged, scooping up the bundle of just-waking baby.

Those emails. . . Will must have received the same amount as the average small business, the time it took him to check them. Twenty minutes later, with Martha slotted in her bouncy chair, I'd cleaned up all the mess, and there was still no sign of Will.

So to relieve the boredom, I was blending. Not teddies and sleepsuits – something marginally more sensible. But only marginally.

"How about this?" I asked Martha, dropping a browning banana – skin and all – into the pinky-orange gloop (an out-of-date raspberry yoghurt and a spoonful of beans from a tub in the fridge).

Martha winced as the blender buzzed and the banana flip-flapped noisily round the glass jug.

"Oooh . . . *this* could make it a good colour!" I said to my sis, as I picked up a dark green bottle of washing up liquid.

I was just about to squirt some in, when I heard signs of life – *alien* life.

Sonny and Kennedy were clattering and chattering through the front door and, by the sounds of it, had gone straight into the living room.

I bristled – I'd very successfully managed to

give my annoying brother a wide berth yesterday (claimed a headache and lurked in my room, where Mum brought me my tea) and this morning (the joys of going to different schools).

Suddenly, the TV was switched on LOUD.

"...*and on* Newsround *today –*"

"...*part of a calorie-controlled diet –*"

"...*this fantastic, genuine diamonique ring could be yours –*"

"...*Ooh, yeah, girl – I'm your maaaaan, baby!!!*"

Sonny was playing flip-around with the remote control, zapping from a kids' telly programme to some ad to a shopping channel to some music channel or other. By the sound of it, he'd settled on the music channel, which would have been all right, if a) it wasn't blasting out some bland-o old boy band type song, and b) it wasn't so stupidly LOUD.

"See the two buttons on the right?!" I said, charging into the living room with Martha on my hip, and grabbing the remote from the arm of the sofa where Sonny had dumped it. "The ones with the up and down arrows? They control the *sound*. You've already done enough damage to Dog, so how about you turn this rubbish down, so it doesn't bust her eardrums?!"

Dog cowered in her cage. Oops – I think my stern growl combined with the telly racket was making things worse.

"Get off my case, Sadie!" Sonny frowned at me, at the same time as the odious, smirking boy band slipped into silence.

"Oooo-OOO-ooo!" I mocked him, as he flounced off in a huff, with the odious, smirking Kennedy in tow.

OK, I was a bit confused. Sonny's response wouldn't normally be to flounce off in a huff. His normal thing would be to grin at me in a deeply frustrating way and say something irritatingly cheeky. This was odd. Still, I got the room to myself . . . which made me think of the *other* room I wanted to get to myself.

"What do you think of pink for the walls?" I asked Martha, as I stomped up the stairs, planning to peek in Dad's former BP and imagine it redecorated. "Not *your* kind of pink. More like *shocking* pink. Do you think that would be cool?"

Why did I slip into using Will's pet word? Maybe because I was passing his and Mum's room right now and could hear him talking on the phone.

". . .*No*, I can't tell her! No way!. . ."

Excuse me?

I took a step backwards with Martha, and held my breath, trying to listen hard (difficult with the The Raconteurs's album blasting out from Sonny's room).

". . .well, it's hardly perfect timing is it? I mean, what am I supposed to say?. . ."

Huh?

"Urgle, urgle, eeee!!"

"Um . . . hold on a sec."

The creak of a bed as Will stood up. Help – I didn't need Martha's baby-speak to blow my ear-wigging cover!

I took a hurried four steps backwards, and put my foot down on to the top stair, so it would hopefully look like I was innocently on my way *upstairs* instead of suspiciously going in *reverse*.

It wasn't till I glanced up in a pink-cheeked fluster that I saw Kennedy in the bathroom doorway, hand on hip, and gazing at me as if I was a complete lunatic. Great.

"Everything OK?" asked Will, coming out on to the landing, and looking as pink-cheeked as me.

"Mmm," I mumbled, feeling very much less than OK.

I'd just cleaned up a big mess single-handedly, ended up looking like a lunatic in front of Sonny's idiot mate and listened into my stepdad having what sounded like a *very* dubious conversation indeed. Hey, I'd had better Monday afternoons.

"Hi, everyone!" Mum trilled from the front door.

Sounded like she'd had a good first day back at school.

"How's it all gone here?" she said, smiling brightly up the stairs at me, Will and Martha. Happy families.

If Will said "cool", I might have to kill him.

"Yeah, cool! No worries!" Will called back, scooping Martha out of my arms and trotting down the stairs to give Mum a welcome home kiss.

Now that I was a baby-free zone, I could go and muck around on my own computer, and research some useful sites on the Internet.

There was *bound* to be one called www.howtokillyourstepdad.com. . .

Amazing, yeah? Yeah, *right*. . .

Guess wot? Stefan Yates just looked at me!!!!!!

Oh dear. . . Letitia's dork of a Fantasy Boyfriend had made eye contact, and now Letitia would be practising her signature in her married name ("Letitia Hermione Yates. . .") and mulling over which Caribbean island they should honeymoon on.

"Anything interesting?" said Dad, opening his front door and spotting me frowning at my text.

"Nope," I replied, stepping inside and quickly firing off an *Oh, yeah? How, where?* to Letty. I wasn't exactly dying to know how and where, but you've got to make an effort with your mates, haven't you?

"Hey, I've been pretty busy, Sadie; wait till you see what I've done!" Dad said proudly.

Well, he must've had a bed for a start. A quick glance towards the bedroom showed no plastic-wrapped mattress, though there did seem to be a

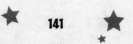

lot of still-packed flat-packs around the hallway from what I could make out. Never mind, they were doubling up nicely as a coat rack at the moment. I slipped off my school blazer and added it to the pile, next to Sonny's denim jacket. He'd beaten me to it, maybe desperate to be first at Dad's for our first official tea here. Whatever, I'd had a pretty nice mosey in the Holloway Road second-hand shop after school. I'd bought myself this vintage Levi's T-shirt, and tried *not* to look at the poster for the sold-out Drop Zone gig at the uni. . .

"Have you ordered a cooker and a washing machine yet?" I asked, following Dad through to the living room, where the telly was blaring out nicely from the surround-sound speakers.

I was ninety-nine-point-nine per cent sure that the answer to my question would be a resounding "er, no".

Dad would probably carry on living on pizza and expect the laundry fairy – otherwise known as Gran – to magically make the grubby clothes all shiny and clean. Poor Gran. After every visit to check on her "boy", she'd be rewarded for her motherly care by trundling back to High Barnet on the tube with a black bin liner of Dad's smelly socks.

"Er, no. Anyway, d'you like it?" said Dad, sweeping away my annoyingly practical question and then sweeping an arm around the living room.

Good grief; with the exception of a new, kitsch, multicoloured plastic beaded curtain at the fire escape door, everything was exactly the same as I'd last seen it on Sunday afternoon. The speakers were still mounted on packing boxes, there was an empty pizza box on the floor (the same one?), and there was still no sofa. So Sonny was once again sprawled on the tan leather armchair, and Cormac (yes, I *know*) was plonked, just like last time, on one of the new folding chairs.

"Have you been superglued there?" I felt like asking Cormac, but didn't.

"Have you adopted him?" I felt like asking my dad, but didn't.

Had I got this wrong? I thought Dad wanted to invite me and Sonny round specially, since this was a fairly momentous milestone – our first (smaller) family meal in his new home. Where did Cormac and his depressing black suit and tie fit in?

"I was just about to go," said Cormac, as if he was reading my mind.

Or maybe he didn't much like me any more after my deliberately sarky comments on Sunday. I might have regretted taking out my grumpy mood on him *and* those sarky remarks if Cormac was a friend or whatever. But he wasn't, and I wasn't exactly in a hurry to get to know him better.

"Here," said Dad, bending down and pressing "stop" on some other comedy DVD they'd obviously all been watching. "Take it and borrow it if you want!"

Dring, dring!

Letitia. Back with more incredibly fascinating details of her deep, meaningful encounter with Stefan Yates.

In newsagent. Looked at me over top of his Nintendo magazine.

Wow, it *must* be love. I had to find out more. Well, I *didn't*, but felt obliged.

Wot then? I keyed in.

"That'd be great!" Cormac was nodding as Dad slotted the DVD into its case. "It might help me get my routine kick-started. I still haven't worked out what I should do. . ."

Not tell jokes would probably be best, I thought, biting my lip as I watched this tall, skinny undertaker look so hopeful and gormless.

"Nah, you want to work out a persona first!" Sonny chipped in, getting all enthused. Uh-oh – here comes some actorly pearls of wisdom. . .

"Huh?" said Cormac, all intrigued.

Please don't encourage him, Sonny, I said silently to myself.

"Well, it's like inventing a part for yourself; based on *you*, obviously, but something sort of exaggerated, maybe. And it makes it a lot easier to get up and perform in front of people if you've got a persona that you psyche yourself into!"

Urgh. Why couldn't I have a nice, normal thirteen-year-old brother who played football, grunted and picked his nose?

"Really?" said Cormac. "But what sort of persona do you think I should. . ."

Dring, dring!

Nuthin, texted Letitia. *He paid for his mag and left. But amazing, yeah?*

Yeah, *right*. . .

I suddenly felt a ripple of pity for Letitia and her useless crush. And sort of sorry for goofy Cormac too, with his useless ambition to be a stand-up comedian, when he had a) no charisma and b) no jokes.

Amazing, I texted back to Letty.

"By the way, Sadie, how's Will?" asked Dad,

drifting away from Sonny and Cormac's buddy-fest.

"Will?" I asked, feeling my cheeks flush a bit at the memory of yesterday's Will weirdness, and that snatch of strange phone call I'd overheard.

"This virus thing he's got," said Dad, frowning at me. "Didn't you know?"

"*What* virus thing?" I asked, confused. I tried to think about what had gone on this morning: shower, breakfast, hi to everyone, cuddle for Dog, Clyde and Martha. The usual. I guess I'd been up and out early; I'd wanted to get the new *NME* magazine and read it before school. It had an interview with The Drop Zone in it, and I thought it would be pretty good to come to Dad's and talk about it this evening. I only vaguely remembered Mum and Will chatting at the kitchen table as I zoomed about, trying to remember what I'd forgotten to pack in my school bag.

"Er . . . I'm not sure what virus. Hold on. MUM!!"

"Yes, Max, dear!" Gran's voice called out from the vicinity of the boxroom.

"You didn't say Gran was here!" I frowned at Dad. Still, it was kind of nice, her being here for this family meal. Actually, she was probably here because she was *cooking* this family meal. Or at least heating it up in Dad's microwave.

Dad and me left the acting masterclass in full flow in the background and headed for the boxroom.

"Hi, Gran!" I smiled from the doorway, since there wasn't room to swing a cat called Dog in this space.

"Well, hello, Sadie, sweetheart!" said Gran, busying herself with something or other, which was her natural state.

My smile faded a little as I glanced at what the busying involved. She was taking Gran-style clothes out of a small suitcase, and putting them in a newly screwed-together IKEA chest of drawers. On top of the chest of drawers was a small vase of freesias, Gran's favourite flowers. They went very well with the new flowery bedspread and the lacy net curtain at the window.

"What's going on?" I asked, sensing that I already knew what was going on.

"Oh, I'm going to stay for a while – help your dad get settled. It'll be lonely for him at first, all on his own," said Gran, as if Dad wasn't in the room, or was a blissfully ignorant five-year-old.

I instantly wanted to shake her for letting herself

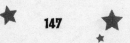

become Dad's personal, unpaid housekeeper, and punch Dad for letting it happen.

"What's this virus thing that Will's got?" Dad asked Gran, oblivious to my shaking/punching urges. "Sadie didn't know anything about it. . ."

"Oh, right!" said Gran. "I've just come from yours, Sadie. Spent a lovely day with Martha. We went to a nursery rhyme singalong at the library this morning, then this afternoon we went for a long walk and had tea and cake at that nice café in Upper Street. What's it called again?"

"You were looking after Martha?" I interrupted her. "So what happened with Will?"

"Oh, it was after your mother left the house – he called me to ask if I could help. He'd been feeling awful since yesterday, he said, but hadn't wanted to say anything to your mother and worry her, what with her just starting back to work."

Oh. Was *that* what that strange snatch of phone call was about? I felt kind of relieved. Except *who* was he talking to?

"Well, I said I'd come straightaway, and Will took himself off to bed," said Gran, pulling a truly *ugg* photo of me and Sonny aged nine out of her bag and sticking it by the new bedside lamp. "He went to the doctor's this afternoon, and they said he's got some virus going around, and that he

needs to rest all week. So of course I'll be looking after Martha. And it's so handy with me staying here!"

Dring, dring!

"S'cuse me, Gran," I muttered, glancing down at my phone, to see what else Letitia had to say about her amazing encounter with her Fantasy Boyfriend.

Meant 2 say, on way 2 newsagent saw Will in café talking to some woman.

I'm sure there was some simple explanation. Maybe the doctor's surgery had unexpectedly burned down after being hit by a random bolt of lightning, and the practice had temporarily moved to the Rendezvous café in Highbury Park. While patient examination and confidentiality was tricky, what with it being a café and all, at least both doctor and patient could discuss symptoms over a nice latte and a chocolate croissant.

Or maybe Will was just up to something he shouldn't have been. . .

15

Just humphing around

You've got to tell someone.
Don't bottle it up.
Share, share, share.

That's what the answers to the problem page letters always say, according to Letitia.

So who to tell about Will's weirdness?

Maybe someone in your family? – that'd be the problem page's first suggestion.

Well, I *couldn't* tell Mum. I mean, hello? "Will is up to some seriously strange stuff, Mum!" That would be one hundred per cent too hard to say, specially if I'd got it all wrong. And anyway, she was ditzier than ever at the moment, hyper-tired from being back at work and on a bit of a low from being away from Martha. (She was sniffling badly as she kissed Martha goodbye this morning, and it wasn't anything to do with the smell wafting from her nappy.)

Dad? Nah. . . I'd decided that definitely felt *too*

weird. He might go and have a word with Mum himself, and how would she take Dad saying something negative about Will? Not great, I bet.

Gran was a no; she'd start hyperventilating and go off on a very loud, slightly hysterical rant, in an even more Irish version of her accent that was practically impossible to understand.

So how about Sonny? Ha! Considering that I was about as close to my twin as I was to the postman, that seemed like a loser of an idea. Plus he'd gone all aloof and sort of grumpy lately, almost like a proper teenage boy should. (Who knew where his annoying hyper-happiness had gone, but I was too stressed out by other stuff to care that much.)

Which left Martha, Clyde and Dog. I *had* tried talking to them, but Martha just dribbled, Clyde washed his ears, and Dog ate her kitty crunchies.

I was left with no alternative.

"What's Will up to? I mean, is he seeing someone? But how could he be seeing someone when he loves my mum, and when his little girl is so . . . little?" I said in a quiet voice, voicing my worst fears.

I'm not sure whether I was actually talking to the Christmas tree, or the dead people out there in the graveyard.

Whatever, the tree waved back and forth above me in the wind, as if it was shrugging, and the slightly higgledy-piggledy gravestones leaned in towards each other, as if their owners below were conferring with each other.

"Well?" I said, hoping for an answer that might make sense, even though it didn't make much sense to ask the question of a hunk of wood and some moss-covered headstones.

"Well, what?" asked Hannah, squeezing through the gap in the railings behind me.

"Just . . . just trying to figure out the Will thing again," I grumbled.

Yep, I'd already told, unbottled and shared, shared, shared with Hannah, and Letty too.

Not that Letty the Problem Page Junkie had been much use; she'd sort of panicked, got stressed that my family was about to fall apart (again) and then asked me how I was feeling seventy-five times a day till I was ready to bookmark www.howtokillyourbestmate.com beside www.howtokillyourstepdad.com.

Hannah had been better; we'd had a few chats on the phone about it (since I was never going to step foot in her house again). But it wasn't till now – late Friday afternoon – that she'd been able to hook up with me.

"Has he still been pretending to be ill?" she asked, tucking long, dark strands of hair behind her ears as she settled herself down on the ground beside me.

"Do you think Will's *pretending?*" I said, all confused. I hadn't thought about that. I'd been fretting about all his mystery phone calls and meetings, and presuming he was genuinely ill at the same time. I mean, why would he pretend to have a virus?

"Well, does *that* look ill to you?" said Hannah, pointing to the bedroom window above the kitchen.

And there was Will, who was supposed to be in bed and resting, animatedly typing away on the laptop that was positioned on the desk by the window.

"He's been in bed for four days now; maybe he's feeling better?" I suggested, noticing Gran dancing out into the garden with Martha on one hip and a laundry basket of damp clothes on the other.

"Yeah, and *maybe* he's using the time to email his secret lover with their secret plans to elope together!" Hannah suggested back, raising her eyebrows archly.

Black humour. Me and Hannah loved that

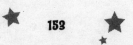

153

stuff, and bantered away dark nonsense all the time. I just wasn't in the mood for it today.

"Only joking!" Hannah said nervously, catching sight of my tense expression. "Hey – have you spoken to your mum about getting your dad's old room yet?"

OK, so that was a very clumsy change of subject, but I was quite glad of a break from my brain grumbling over the Will weirdness.

"Sort of. I spoke to her last night. . ."

I'd finally caught Mum on her own – hard to do in my house – just after she'd put Martha to bed.

"Mum?" I'd said, watching her scrabble through a ton of sheet music in her propped-open piano stool. At her feet, a pile of paperwork and scrawled teaching plans spilled out from her bag across the floor. Clyde was nibbling at the edge of a green cardboard folder that was probably full of something vital.

"Yes, honey?" said Mum absently, giving me a quick, sweet smile before she dropped her head down again. "Go on – I'm listening. Just got to find a piece of music I want to take in tomorrow for one of my students. . ."

"Dad's old room—"

"Oh! Don't talk to me about it! It's such a

mess, still!" Mum sighed, shaking her head and sending her hair tumbling. "When's he going to move the last bits and pieces?"

"I dunno. Anyway, I was thinking, maybe I could move into it?"

"Mmm, maybe. . ." Mum muttered, holding up a printed sheet of paper and frowning at it. "I can't bear to look in there. When you next see him, can you ask him when he's popping back for the rest of the clutter?"

"Yeah, OK. So what to you think?"

"WaaaaaaahhhhhhhhhhhhhHHHHHHHHHHH HHHHHHH!"

Like a fireman jumping into action at the sound of a siren, Mum bolted from her seat to attend the urgent Martha emergency, which probably involved wind, or the fact that her thumb couldn't find her mouth in the dark.

And so that was my "sort of" discussion about the room with Mum. After that, she'd been snuggled on the sofa with Will, which – in the current climate – made me feel so *un*snuggly that I'd scooped up Clyde and gone to my room. On the way there, I'd paused outside Sonny's not-quite-shut door – I could hear some serious thumping around going on in there. Maybe someone was beating him up? Of course it wasn't anything as exciting as that; through the sliver of a crack, I could make out the big dork humphing around doing some stupid stage school dance moves to whatever music he was listening to on his white iPod headphones.

Of course, he spotted me (hey, Gran – maybe it was some spooky sixth sense!) and booted the door shut in my face. Nice.

So I'd spent the rest of the evening making Clyde bond with my evil rabbit bandaged fingers by feeding him chunks of carrot with my injured hand. He'd ended up going to sleep cuddled up against it, which was very lovely, except that I was tired and didn't want to disturb him, so I woke up on the bedroom floor at four-thirty in the morning with a crick in my neck.

"It'll be great when you move in there!" said Hannah, gazing up at the window of the garage room.

Hmm.

I felt so freakily uncomfortable at home right now that I was semi-jealous of Gran making herself at home in Dad's horrid box of a room above the undertaker's. . .

Spot the big faker

It was a real love story; they got together through mutual hatred.

I know, I know. My ditzy mum Nicola and Mr "Cool!" Will. Neither of them were the hate-filled type (though Mum might be soon, if my deepest fears about Will turned out to be true. . .).

But anyway, that's how it was. Mum – who understood sport as much as she understood Nu Rave music (i.e. not at all) – and Will – who understood classical music about as much as Martha and Clyde the rabbit did – bonded in the staffroom when they both realized how much they despised the head teacher of the school they worked for.

The head teacher thought that music and sport were about as useful as a marshmallow frying pan, and liked everyone in Mum and Will's respective departments to know that. What departments they had *left* to work in, that is, since he kept cutting their budgets and making their colleagues redundant.

So over biscuits and uncharacteristic moaning, Mum and Will fell for each other, and the rest is blah, blah, blah. There was love, there was moving in, there was the joy of Martha being born and the horrible head teacher thankfully retiring, and things couldn't get much better. Till now, when they might be about to get quite a lot *worse*.

"For you, Nicola," said Will, pulling a bunch of pretty something-or-other flowers out from behind the newspaper and milk he'd just been out to fetch this Saturday morning.

Yeah, and while he was on a secret assignation, rendezvousing with his paramour. Maybe.

"Oh, Will!" Mum gushed, tenderly taking the something-or-others and sniffing at them. Breastfeeding below, Martha must have caught a whiff of pollen and gave a kitten-y sneeze.

"I'm sorry about this week, Nicola – I didn't mean to stress you out on top of starting back at work!"

She'd be a lot more stressed out if she knew about all the Will weirdness, I thought to myself, as I grabbed some yoghurt to have for breakfast from out of the fridge.

"You couldn't help it, honey!" Mum smiled up at Will.

Ha – couldn't he?

"And anyway, Joan was perfectly happy to help out," Mum assured him, talking about Gran, of course.

"Yeah, and Martha *does* adore her grandma. . ." Will agreed.

Um, *non*-grandma, technically, don't forget. Though I wasn't disputing the adoring bit.

"Just going outside to have this," I muttered, holding up my yoghurt and heading out into the glorious sunshine of the garden.

Mum and Will seemed too loved-up to notice that I'd even been in the kitchen with them, never mind that I'd said anything. (The loved-up thing; was that the sign of a man who was cheating? I didn't think so, but I couldn't know for sure. Being thirteen and never having had a boyfriend kind of limits your range of knowledge, I had to admit.)

Anyway, on to some pleasantly distracting stuff: when I got out into the garden, Clyde was staring at a line of ants. Excellent. Ants and food of any kind are always great for passing the time. Five minutes later, and the ants were negotiating an exciting and testing obstacle course of twigs, clothes pegs, a garden trowel and a feathery cat toy as they tried to reach the blob of blackcurrant yoghurt I'd dribbled on the path for them to find.

"Which one are you betting on to be first?" I asked Clyde, who was tentatively giving the moving line of ants a lick, as if he was mulling over the possibility of ditching his vegetarian ways.

Creak!!

I gazed up at the familiar-ish sound coming from above the garage.

It was a window opening – the stiff one in Dad's former BP.

"What are you doing?" I shouted up at Sonny, who was loitering in the window frame. Helping gather up the last of Dad's tat maybe? He was picking us both up soon, so the three of us could hang out together for the afternoon.

"Well, just trying to clear the place up a bit," Sonny said with a shrug. "Then Will's going to help me move my stuff in here later."

If looks could kill, Sonny would be an incinerated pile of ashes by now and he knew it.

"What?!" He frowned down at me.

Straight away, I sussed out what had happened: Sonny had listened in again. (Just like last Saturday, when he heard me telling Mum about the practical joke disater at Hannah's house.)

He must have listened in on me asking Mum for the room, and gone in with his own – terribly *innocent* – request to have it. Possibly at a time when Mum didn't have music playing in her head and drowning everything else out.

"Get *out* of there! *I* asked for that room first!!" I squealed in a more girly way than I meant to. At the same time, I scrabbled to my feet and accidentally squashed a few ants in the process. (Sorry, guys.)

Sonny disappeared from the window. From inside the house I could hear his muffled shout of "Mum! Sadie said I have to get out 'cause. . ."

I didn't wait for the rest – I stomped back into the kitchen and shoved my hands on my hips.

Ouch.

"Mum!! *Why* is Sonny moving into the garage room?" I demanded, shaking my twingingly sore bandaged fingers.

"Well, uh, because it's quite big, and he has all his dance moves to practise," said Mum, a little confused and shell-shocked at my obvious rage. "Why?"

"Because *I* asked you about it *first*!!" I said, trying not to let angry tears prickle at my eyes.

"Did you?" Mum blinked dippily. "When did—"

Rappity-rappity rap! Ding-dong, ding-dong!!

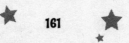

"OK if I come in?" Dad hollered from the front door.

"Course, Max!" Mum called back. "C'mon through – we're in the kitchen!"

"Great news!!" Dad bellowed, as if we were in his work unit two streets away instead of ten *paces* away. "Where's Sonny? SONNY!!"

Cue thunder of feet from above – Sonny had decided it was safe to stop hiding upstairs now that he reckoned Dad's entrance had defused my fury.

"Sadie!" said Dad, turning to me, after patting Will on the back, pecking Mum on the cheek, and ruffling Martha's virtually non-existent hair. "Remember there was a competition on the radio, the day you and Dog came by?"

"Uh-huh," I said through gritted teeth, my fury only interrupted, not defused.

"Well, I won!" said Dad, holding out a fistful of bits of paper.

"Cool!" exclaimed Will, even though he had as much (make that as *little*) idea of what Dad was on about as the rest of us.

"Six – count 'em! – *six* tickets to see The Drop Zone at the University of North London tomorrow *night*!!!"

OK, consider my bad mood shelved, if not gone.

The Drop Zone! I was actually going to see them play live! I could wear that new vintage Levi's T-shirt! My dad wasn't such a useless, music-obsessed anorak after all!!

"Wow, Dad!" said Sonny, barrelling in for a bear hug.

"Fantastic, Max!" Mum beamed, even though she hadn't a clue who The Drop Zone were, since her all her favourite music was composed before the 1850s.

"Who's coming, then, Dad?" I asked. There'd be me and Sonny, of course. The others would be some of Dad's mates; maybe even Daryl and/or Kemal from work, who were pretty all right.

"Well, *me*, obviously, since *I'm* the hero who won the tickets!" Dad joked around. "Then I thought one for Kennedy—"

"Yay!" shouted Sonny. "I'll go and phone him right now!"

"—and I've already asked Cormac, 'cause I met him when he was unloading a coffin outside the shop today, so that leaves—"

Cormac? Urgh. . . After niggling so nastily at him, I knew he wouldn't want to socialize with me. And I didn't have any burning desire to socialize with *him*.

"Max!" I heard Mum interrupt Dad. "What

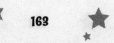

about *Will* having that last ticket? He loves music, and he's had a rough week with this virus. . ."

"Of course!" said Dad, shrugging his shoulders at Mum's suggestion. "The more the merrier!"

"Um, if you're sure that's cool, Max?" Will checked with my dad.

"Absolutely!" said Dad, giving Will another manly thump on the arm.

"Cool," said Will, with a broad smile, acting like hanging out with Dad was a rare treat indeed.

The big faker.

And now I was starting to stress that Will might be faking a whole lot more than just a matey fondness for my dad.

The flowers and the apologies and the love-up look; was he faking it with Mum too. . .?

Mesmerized by strange socks

What's with Japanese girls and strange socks?

I'd seen this freaky fashion heaps of times in places like Covent Garden in the West End of London, or trendy Camden Market.

And now a bunch of five girls to the left of us, standing on their tip-toes – trying to catch a glimpse of the band – were *really* going for it in the strange sock stakes.

Get this:

- One pair of pink, fishnet pop socks, worn with yellow trainers
- One pair of stripy socks with individual toe sections, like gloves for your feet, worn with wooden wedges
- One pair of black leg warmers with lace at the knee, worn with Birkenstocks
- One pair of green ankle socks, consisting of

only the *ankle* bit, worn barefoot with black ballet pumps
- One pair of black and silver speckled socks, consisting of only the *toe* section, worn with strappy sandals

I was transfixed. I'd been obsessing about The Drop Zone for weeks now, and here I was, mesmerized by strange socks and forgetting about the four blokes on stage, thrashing away at their instruments.

But it wasn't just the socks. My concentration was shot; I didn't know why. Actually I did – I'd have been enjoying the band a whole lot more if the people I was here with weren't annoying me so much.

"See how he's holding the audience?" Sonny was booming away so loudly that, despite the music, not only Cormac and Kennedy could hear him, but everyone within a two-metre radius.

Cormac nodded. He'd been nodding like a stupid nodding dog toy for the last fifteen minutes, i.e. ever since The Drop Zone had come on stage. At first it had been in time to the music, and then it had been in time to everything Sonny was saying. I wanted to reach over, clamp his head still, and remind him that Sonny was only thirteen years old, and seventeen-year-old Cormac didn't have to take *everything* he said as gospel.

"It's totally about stage presence," Sonny was blabbing on.

"Totally," Kennedy repeated loudly. Kennedy was good at repeating stuff loudly. He seemed to think that if he did that enough, people might think *he'd* come up with whatever the original thought was, instead of being a wide-faced, shallow-brained parrot.

"Like I was saying the other day, he's got a persona," Sonny said continuing his mission to be Cormac's performance coach. "You can bet Ewan isn't as serious and intense off-stage. It's just his act!"

"Yeah, just his act!" Kennedy shrugged.

I looked at Ewan, the serious and intense lead singer of The Drop Zone, and reckoned he was *exactly* like that off-stage. In his interview in the *NME* last week, he'd listed his hobbies as listening to records made by people who were dead or depressed and reading books by political dissidents. I didn't even know what a political dissident *was*, but it didn't sound like they'd write books with lots of funny bits in them.

Why did Sonny have to be such a know-all, even about stuff he didn't *know* about?!

"Trouble is, I still don't know what persona to go for," Cormac suddenly said, taking a break from nodding his head loose.

I couldn't stop myself, I really couldn't.

"You don't *need* some fancy *persona*. You just need to have the right *material*, and enough *bottle*!" I jumped in and said, thinking of The Drop Zone and their attitude and their album's worth of killer tracks. In my head, that translated as "*You* don't have any material, *or* the bottle, do you?". Cormac somehow seemed to know that, and sort of withered under my gaze, even though he was at least ten centimetres taller than me.

"Hey, it's more than that!" Sonny contradicted.

"Yeah, it's more than that!" Kennedy parroted.

"What are you *talking* about?" I said directly to Sonny. I guess I was just extra mad at him for nicking the room that was rightfully mine. "You're giving advice and it's not like you've ever done anything that amazing! It not like you've ever . . . I dunno. . ."

I found myself pointing at The Drop Zone as an example.

". . .gone into the Top Ten of the charts with your first CD or whatever!"

"Yeah?! Just you *wait*!!" bellowed Kennedy.

Y'know, I think I preferred Kennedy when he

was being a parrot to when he was being an idiot.

"Shut up!" said Sonny, irately.

I thought he was talking to me, and then realized he was talking to Kennedy, but, whatever, I couldn't be bothered with this dumb conversation any more, so I shuffled forward into the space between Dad and Will, and instantly regretted it.

"All right, Sadie?" Dad said brightly, his eyes glued to the stage and oblivious to anything going on behind him.

Dad, Dad, Dad. Thanks for winning the tickets and everything, but *whoa* . . . what was with the posing? Honestly, he'd gone to town with the hair wax and had the loud '50s Hawaiian shirt. The loud '50s Hawaiian shirt that he'd left *one* too many buttons undone on, as if his manly chestliness would make any female Drop Zone fans – or maybe the cluster of Japanese students with their strange socks – drool with lust. OK, *maybe* the quirky look might have worked if he was two or three decades younger, three stone lighter and his hair wasn't receding. . .

I knew that thinking this stuff was less than kind, and, hey, Dad, deserved to find a new someone sometime, same as Mum had done. I just didn't want to be around to watch him make a fool of himself while he was doing it.

Wish Hannah and Letitia were here with me instead, I said silently to myself. But then again, Hannah would probably embarrass me by wearing her Radiohead T-shirt and looking blankly at any Radiohead fans who might try and talk to her about it. And thinking about it, I bet Letitia would find the crowd and the darkness and the loudness too much and embarrass me by asking to go home five seconds after we arrived. . .

So what about Will?

I scowled at him from the corner of my eye, trying to read his big faker mind.

He was staring straight at the band, clutching a bottle of beer in one hand so tightly that his knuckles were white, and furiously biting the nails on his other hand. He looked *completely* stressed out, like he was watching a *train* wreck instead of a rock band.

What was with him?!

"What's *wrong*?"

I didn't think about it; it came right out. Maybe the loud, thrashing music gave me the confidence to ask Will a straight question.

Though he was probably was going to fake it

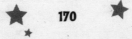

all over again and say, "Nothing! Everything's cool!".

Will turned to face me, *seemed* as if he was about to say something (probably "Nothing! Everything's cool!"), and then stopped. His shoulders sank, his face fell.

"Sadie. . . can we go up to the back for a second, where it's quieter? I really need to talk to you."

Cue my stomach plummeting from the centre of my body to the soles of my slip-on Converse trainers. . .

18

Payback time

". . .*Oh, my Rose of Traleeeeeee!!*" trilled Gran, with a warble in her voice and a dirty nappy in her hand.

"Eeee-oooo-eeeee!!" Martha gurgled happily, waving her pink legs and hands in the air.

Will scribbled frantically in a small notebook, determined – in his mildly obsessive-compulsive way – to be the best dad possible. It was as if he was studying for his A-level in Fatherly Excellence.

I stopped scratching Dog through the bars of her cage and leant over a little to see what exactly Will had written down.

SUBJECT: NAPPIES. Sing to Martha when changing nappy.
(Get Joan to teach me some Irish folk songs??)

See what I mean? Will was a major stress-head when it came to details. I'd always known that,

but I hadn't realized quite how *much* of a stress-head he actually was. And hurray for his impressive faking skills; I really, truly didn't know how completely terrified he'd been of looking after Martha on his own and doing stuff wrong. Hence a day's masterclass with a woman who just *loved* to be useful.

By the way, it was a *secret* masterclass, which Gran seemed to get a buzz from.

"Now don't you worry, Sadie, darling," she'd said, when I'd slipped out of the hall and into the corridor at the uni gig last night and called her. "I'll not say a word. It'll all be fine. Just you tell that young man that I'll be there at 8.30 a.m. sharp tomorrow morning!"

I'd gone back to the bar, where Will's knuckles were a less vivid shade of white as he clutched the bottle, but his eyes still looked hunted and desperate. I gave him the thumbs-up.

"She'll do it!" I'd said softly as I got up close, in case Dad or Sonny or the others had followed us on our (fake) mission to get more drinks.

At least, that'd been Will's cover for taking me away for that ominous sounding talk. The talk where he'd admitted he'd practically been getting an *ulcer* the last few weeks, as he'd mega-fretted about being all-day Daddy. Oh, yeah.

173

That was the reason behind all of Will's weirdness.

The middle-of-the-night food-fest? Him panicking, and practising making baby gloop.

The nail-biting? Pure nerves.

The "call you if you need me" message on his leaving card? It was from Leah, the part-time receptionist at his school, mum of a nine-month-old sprog called Paris-Jade (I *know*) and the only person Will had confided in, who'd promised she'd be on the end of a phone, if he needed to find out which end to put a nappy on.

The odd behaviour in the bookshop, when he should have been at the supermarket? He'd met up with Leah, who'd been coaching him on good Baby DIY books. He'd hidden his chosen book, and waved a half-hidden bye to Leah when he nearly got rumbled by me and a squalling Martha.

The trashed living room that first Monday? Will's stressed-out mess, and not Martha's, though I'd pretty much suspected that. (The mess must have been a pretty tough admission of failure for tidy-freak Will.)

The whispered phone message I'd overheard? Poor Leah, getting hassled for help again.

Letitia spotting him in the café that wasn't a

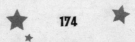

doctor's surgery? Ah, Letitia hadn't spotted baby Paris-Jade asleep in her buggy, or this Leah person's strained face at yet *another* baby pep-talk.

The virus? Made up – a way for Will to stall for time. He'd been on the laptop in the bedroom every day, anxiously researching lots of parenting websites for tips, but getting more petrified by the millisecond when he saw the lists of problems and whinges that mums had posted on them.

"Uh-oh. Has she got a bit of nappy rash, there?" said Will, all a-flutter with concern, and pointing the end of his pencil at three tiny spots on Martha's pudgy bottom.

"Well, a *little* bit." Gran shrugged matter-of-factly, while gently shoo-ing Clyde away from the packet of baby wipes he was about to nibble.

"So what do I do about that?" asked Will, his brows all furrowed.

"What do you do normally, when Nicola's here?" Gran asked him patiently, the way the teachers at school always answer a question with a question, just to force you to think (more's the pity).

"Um . . . put on some of this?" said Will, holding up a pot of nappy rash cream.

"Well, *that's* what you do, then," Gran said sagely, as Will began to scribble orders to himself in his notebook.

Clink, CLUNK!!

The sound of keys in the door – we all froze.

"Sadie, run and put the kettle on, and I'll say I just popped by for a nice cup of tea and a catch-up!" Gran ordered me hurriedly, since she'd been too busy coaching Will all day to think of an excuse for her presence when Mum came home from work. (Which was a bit of a joke really, since Gran was *always* at our house anyway, and hardly needed an excuse for it.)

I tried to hurry myself up, but sore fingers and the stiff school blazer that I hadn't yet taken off kind of hampered me a bit.

"Hi. . ." said a flat-ish voice, a voice that belonged to Sonny, and not Mum after all. Phew.

"Hey, Sonny. Good day at school?" Will called through to him, as he shoved his notebook into the back pocket of his jeans.

"Mmm," mumbled Sonny, coming and hovering at the living-room door.

"Can I get you a snack there, Sonny?" Gran asked him, flipping into catering mode.

"No. . . I'm going to go upstairs and go over some stuff for school while it's in my head," he

muttered, throwing his rucksack up on to his shoulder and trundling towards the stairs.

"Got a performance coming up?" asked Gran. "Or is it an audition?"

"Yeah, something like that," Sonny said vaguely, before shuffling off.

"Righto," Gran called uncertainly after him, before lowering her voice to talk to me. "What's Sonny got on at school at the moment? He's not been talking much about it the last week or so. . ."

Ah, she'd noticed too.

Actually, now that the strain of the Will weirdness had disappeared, I found myself once again mildly concerned about Sonny's lack of day-to-day showing-off.

"Don't know, Gran," I said with a shrug. "Remember, I *never* know what's going on with Sonny."

With that, I got up to flip on the kettle, and get some food ready for Dog and Clyde.

But after a couple of minutes pottering in the kitchen, my rebellious and curious feet turned in the direction of the stairs, and I found myself quietly walking up them, as if I were going to the loo.

The loo that was just next to Sonny's new room. The room that had been cleaned and

painted by Will and Sonny on Saturday, and moved into yesterday, before we went to the gig.

Now then. . . It suddenly occurred to me that in the barging-in stakes, I'd never got payback for the walking-in-on-me-in-my-undies episode of a couple of weeks ago.

And so I felt it was high time for a no-knocking moment. Maybe I'd walk in on Sonny rehearsing squeezing spots for a teen acne cream ad. . .

"Hey, have you got my Magic Numbers CD?" I said, thinking up an excuse on the spot as I breezed into Dad's former BP.

Ah. Now it appeared to be Sonny's ROS: his Room Of Shame. . .

"What DO you look like?" I gasped.

Sonny stopped dead, frozen in front of the long mirror he used to check his dance moves in, and how "gorgeous" he was looking.

Though looking gorgeous wasn't exactly on the agenda now. I'd caught Sonny pouring himself into a pair of hideous, purple-with-yellow-side-striped cycling shorts, made out of shiny Lycra. Skinny as he was in general, thanks to his dance practice, the muscles in his thighs were pretty chunky. The tops of his legs looked like psychedelic sausages.

"You're supposed to *knock* – that's the *rule!*" Sonny said, blushing.

How funny; I'd never seen him embarrassed about *any* outfit before – and remember, I'd seen him dressed as a fairy in *A Midsummer's Night's Dream* when he was in a local drama group, an Ewok in an improvised *Star Wars* scene at stage school, and a nit for a magazine ad for a headlice shampoo.

"Well, let's call it one-all – and let's *both* remember in the future!" I couldn't help smirking as I headed back into the corridor and pulled the door shut behind me.

OK, so it was a bit of revenge, not only for the bra-and-pants thing, but for getting in and nicking the room from under me.

Revenge was sweet, though it would have been sweeter if I'd thought to barge in with my camera phone and capture the moment, so I could torture him with it for infinity.

Can you imagine? Every time Sonny went to open his mouth and bug me, I could hold up the screen of my phone and silence him with one swift, cringeworthy image.

Whoever said blackmail was a totally *bad* thing. . .?

19

www.howtokillsonnybird.com

Dog purred, and nuzzled her plastic collar into my side, delirious to have close-up company.

"You all right in there, Sadie?" asked Mum, breaking off from bouncing Martha on her knee. "It looks like a bit of a squash..."

"It's fine," I said, tilting my head a little to the left, so that it didn't press quite so uncomfortably into the metal bars of the top of the cage. "Five more weeks to go, eh?"

I said that more to Dog than Mum, but Mum "mmm"d in agreement anyway.

"Hnnnuuuuh, hnuuuuuuuuh..."

"Oh! What *is* it, sweetie?" Mum frowned as Martha switched from bouncily happy to unfathomably whiny.

Will strode into the room and held out his arms to scoop up my cute kid sis.

"Here... give her to me," he said confidently, without a trace of fakeness in his voice or manner,

thanks to his (shhhh) excellent training all this week. He wandered off with Martha in his arms, whistling "Danny Boy", slightly out of tune.

"Sadie, darling, I *have* been meaning to say sorry properly for the business about the garage room," Mum suddenly said, running a hand through her prettily dishevelled dark hair.

I shrugged. "It's OK." I knew it wasn't a hundred per cent Mum's fault. Let's call it *forty* per cent, for her inability to switch off the music in her head and concentrate when people were trying to talk to her, while I'd say *sixty* per cent of the blame lay with my irritating brother for grabbing it for himself – when I was *ninety* per cent sure he knew I'd asked *first*.

"You could always have *Sonny's* old room, you know?" Mum suggested. "I mean, it *is* bigger than the one you're in just now. . ."

Hmm. I didn't really think I wanted anything hand-me-down and second-best of Sonny's. Even if it *was* a room twice the size of mine, with a great view over the garden and the cemetery and the asylum-seeking Christmas tree hidden in the mini-wood. . .

"Sadie!" said the room-grabber, all of a sudden strutting into the living room, holding on to the phone. "Got Dad on the line – instead of going round to his today, he says he wants us to meet him on Highbury Fields in half an hour's time. He says to bring friends if we want. He says he's got a surprise."

Uh-oh – last time Dad had a surprise, it involved dead bodies. I hoped this one was an improvement. Whatever it was, from the smirk on Sonny's face, he already knew about it. Grrr.

"Give me the phone – let me talk to Dad," I said, struggling to get Dog's contented claws out of my jeans and wriggle myself out of the clanking cage door.

"Yeah, Sadie says fine. See you, then. Bye!" Sonny babbled hastily, before clicking the off button. "Sorry! Dad said he was in a hurry. . ."

Grr again.

Could it be at all possible that someone else had put together a website called www.howtokill sonnybird.com yet?

If they hadn't, it was about time. . .

"What's his name again?" asked Hannah, her arms folded across the lettering of her Gorillaz T-shirt.

"Cormac. Cormac McConnell," I replied, really, *really* not sure what was going on.

"What's the box for?" asked Letitia.

"I have no idea," I told her.

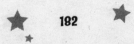

Cormac – in his best black funeral suit and tie – was standing right behind a small wooden crate. I was sure that the last time I'd seen that small wooden crate, it had a collection of Dad's old 45-inch singles in it.

Speaking of Dad, the way he was dressed (pink and white Hawaiian shirt) was clashing a bit with Cormac's outfit. It was like Bart Simpson hanging out with a High Court judge.

"Why do we have to stand right here?" asked Hannah.

"I've no idea."

I really didn't. When we got to the park and the bottom end of Highbury Fields, as directed by Dad, my brother Sonny and his less-than-lovely buddy Kennedy had already beaten us to it, along with Dad, Cormac and his mystery box. And Dad had asked us girls to stand at this particular point, a few grassy metres away, so that's what me and my friends were doing, though we had absolutely *no* clue why.

"What's happening?"

That wasn't Hannah or Letitia – that was a couple of guys in their thirties, out walking their sausage dog in the park.

"I've no idea," I said, feeling like I might be repeating myself.

"What're Sonny and Kennedy and your dad saying to Cormac?" asked Letitia.

You know, I watched a programme on TV once, where they showed clips of ultra famous people like the Queen or Elton John or the president of the United Nations chatting in the background, and then got a lip-reading expert in to explain that the famous person had said something like, "Ooh, I could *murder* a burger!" or something brilliantly banal like that.

I wished I could hire an instantaneous lip reader now, so I could figure out what was going on. But maybe I wouldn't have to. Maybe I could find out quicker than I expected. Sonny, Kennedy and Dad were walking across the grass towards us, leaving Cormac, his funeral suit and his wooden box on their own.

"So?" I said to Dad.

"So, Cormac's got a surprise for you!" Dad beamed, as more Saturday morning park strollers began hovering around us and making a small crowd.

"For *me*?!" I said, feeling myself flush as much as Cormac seemed to be flushing right now, directly above his stiff white collar and below his bright red spiky hair.

"I've been coaching him all week," Sonny

butted in, proud as a peacock over whatever it was he'd coached Cormac to do.

"I've been helping," Kennedy blurted, like I needed to know that.

"He's not going to do a solo out of *Swan Lake*, is he?" I said, looking directly at Sonny (why waste eye muscles on Kennedy?). I could tell that my lop-sided grin was all snarly since my words were so loaded with sarcasm.

"He's doing a stand-up comedy spot." Dad smiled. "Inspired by *you*, Sadie!"

Hannah and Letitia – whatever their differences – both threw me a "wow!" sort of look. I blanked them, panicking slightly about what was going on. Or *about* to go on. Cormac was placing one and then two feet on the wooden box.

"What-d'you-mean?" I burbled at high speed, feeling a pinking of panic flushing my cheeks.

Dad grinned. "It's nothing *bad*. It's just that you sort of spurred Cormac on, Sadie."

"Huh?" I sensed the pinking spreading down my neck. I couldn't think *how* I could have spurred Cormac on to do anything, since I hadn't been particulary nice to him in any way.

Help . . . he wasn't going to throw a cream pie in my face or something, was he?

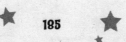

"Well," Dad continued, "Cormac told me after the gig on Sunday night that he felt you thought he couldn't do it. Stand-up, I mean. And I guess that made him want to prove you wrong!"

Urgh. Was I supposed to feel chuffed by that? Or horrified that I'd been so negative that Cormac had desperately wanted to prove me wrong?

Double urgh . . . there was *definitely* a custard pie headed my way, for sure. And it was coming any minute now.

Worse still, I probably deserved it. . .

Cormac was coughing, like he was about to start. At least fifteen to twenty people were mooching around, dying to see what this cartoony-looking red-headed guy in the weird suit was about to say (or do).

Make it be funny, please make it be funny, I found myself begging silently.

Suddenly, I didn't care if there was a pie with my name on it; I couldn't stand the idea of Cormac standing there telling a string of dumb jokes and shrivelling up in front of a row of unsmiling faces. He seemed to be an OK guy, who hadn't deserved to have me growl at him, when really it was my stupid brother who I was annoyed at.

I wanted to radiate good vibes and good luck to Cormac. Though that was pretty hard to do since my whole body was tensed in an almighty cringe on his behalf.

"Hello!" said Cormac brightly, and slightly awkwardly. "My name is Cormac McConnell, and I'm a trainee funeral director."

Hey, that was quite an opening line. The rag-tag group gathered around either stared, mouths agape, or gave him a cheer and round of applause for that strange and unexpected admission.

"Now *some* people might think this is a strange job for a seventeen-year-old guy to have. . ."

A ripple of laughter.

". . .especially *one* person I know – who I'll call *Zadie*, to protect her privacy, since she's here today!"

Another ripple of expectant laughter.

Um . . . this didn't sound much like the start of a string of dumb jokes. What exctly was going on here?

"Sadie! He means *you*!" Letitia "whispered" too loudly as she nudged me with her elbow. I didn't look at her. Or Dad, or Sonny, or Hannah. I kept my gaze straight ahead, aimed at Cormac, as I tried to zone out any faces turned towards me.

"Anyway, my friend *Zadie*—"

I wasn't so sure about sending him good vibes any more. In fact, I felt like heckling him, shouting, "Y'know, *technically* she's NOT your friend!". But of course I didn't.

Actually, someone else did.

"Oi, Ginge! Going to a funeral?" some drongo yelped.

A drongo all sweaty from a game of tennis on the courts further up Highbury Fields. A drongo who looked – to some – like a member of Westlife.

"Oh! *That's* not nice!" gasped Letitia, who'd suffered a few snidey, ignorant digs at her expense over the years – 'cause of the colour of her skin – and felt *very* anti people being picked on because of how they looked. I noticed her frowning hard at her instantly ex-Fantasy Boyfriend. Plenty of other people were staring at Stefan Yates in the same way. He'd have probably got the message from the shut-up, disapproving glances going on, but Cormac got right in there anyway.

"No, actually, I'm *not* due to attend a funeral this afternoon, but you be careful crossing the road on your way home, yeah? 'Cause I wouldn't want you to be my next client!"

Bursts of laughter and a round of applause. More people in the park were drifting towards us, just as Stefan Yates was skulking away, tail between his legs.

I might have been quite proud of Cormac, if I wasn't so worried about what was coming next.

"Anyway, before we were so rudely interrupted," Cormac carried on, sounding surprisingly confident, even if his slight blush gave him away a bit, "I was telling you about *Zadie*. Well, my friend *Zadie* has a real problem with the job I do. She thinks it's deeply *weird*."

"Brilliant! It *is* you he's speaking about, isn't it?" Hannah whispered in my left ear.

Yeah-*huh*!! Did she reckon?!

"Thing is, I think she should look at her *own* life first before she goes dissing *mine*."

My head started to spin. I think it was the lack of oxygen, since I wasn't particularly *breathing* all of a sudden. This was turning into a cream pie, all right – a verbal one.

"Get this; is this normal? *Zadie* has a cat she named *Dog*."

Laughter.

"It gets worse. When *Zadie* gets bored, she does some pretty interesting stuff to keep herself entertained. Like one time, she tried to turn

Dog – that's a *cat*, remember – into a robot by wrapping it up in silver foil."

More laughter. Less breathing from me. *Dad* must have told him that story.

"Never mind the cat called Dog – she's also got a rabbit that she lets live in the house, that she's trained to use a *litter* tray. What next? Is she going to teach it to record telly programmes when she's out? Or help it learn how to make risotto and a fine mushroom linguine in its spare time, when it's not busy lolloping around?"

Giggles and guffawing all around.

"And *Zadie* – who thinks *I'm* weird, remember – also has a very special childhood friend who she shares all her troubles with. It's a two-metre tall Christmas tree that lives in the graveyard next to her house."

Lots more laughter. I felt like I might keel over. I think I'd have preferred him to just reel off that stream of dumb jokes that nobody laughed at.

"He's quite funny, isn't he?" Letitia whispered in my right ear, in that breathy voice she tended to use when she was talking about a future Fantasy Boyfriend. Uh-oh.

"Now, *Zadie*, she recently busted her hand. But it wasn't in any way you might expect, like falling off skis, or a skateboard or even a bike."

My hand – with its new plaster tape on since the "rabbit" bandage went in the wash – flew instantly into my pocket.

"Nope – she fell off the side of a bath. Hey, it's an everyday occurence that could happen to any of us – *not*."

Laughter, laughter, laughter.

"I mean, someone secretly lays cling film across the loo, you innocently do what you have to do and – whoops! – it goes *everywhere*; you've got nothing to clean up the mess with, so you stand on the edge of the bath to reach some spare loo roll and find yourself slipping off, and landing face down in a puddle of your own wee, with a broken hand. *That's* the kind of stuff that happens in *Zadie's* world. And she thinks *mine's* strange?"

"Sorry, Sadie – it was just too funny not to tell to him!" Dad apologized, wrapping a pink-and-white arm round me. (What was worse: having a funeral director retell your most embarrassing moments in front of strangers, or have all these strangers know that the bloke in the loud Hawaiian shirt was my dad?)

"And wait, this is the best bit. This *Zadie*, right, is pretty smart, and knows everything about everything –"

Oh, a sort of compliment, I realized with surprise.

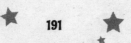

"– but the joke is, there's something she *doesn't* know: her own twin brother has the hugest of all secrets, and he's too scared to tell her!"

Bang went the nice post-compliment feeling. What fresh embarrassment was headed my way?

And check it out; the ever-grinning Sonny had now turned around to face me, but he wasn't grinning any more. I'd guess that *this* bit of Cormac's repertoire wasn't something Sonny had helped him rehearse.

Me and my brother both shot a "what's going on?" glance at Dad, who just shrugged back, as uncertain as us where this was going.

"This *Zadie*, right, hates – I mean *hates* boy bands. So it's probably going to be a bit of a surprise to her to know that her own twin brother – let's call him *Donny* – has just auditioned and been accepted to join a – you guessed it, folks, a *boy* band!!"

Yep, I didn't know that stuff.

Yep, I was as weird as Cormac was making out in his stand-up routine.

Yep, I had a childhood friend who happened to be a tree, and I wanted to hang out with it right now.

"Sadie. . .?" I heard Dad say, but I was suddenly running as fast as my DIY slip-on trainers would let me. . .

A grouch like me

I was lying flat down, hands folded across my chest, mulling over how peaceful, serene and un-embarrassing it must feel to be dead.

Unless you died in a *stupid* way, of course, like by being mown down by a runaway ice-cream van. Or choking on candyfloss. Or being humiliated to death in a public park by someone you vaguely know. . .

"Hey," said Sonny.

I kept my eyes closed. To the best of my knowledge, the last time Sonny had come out here to the mini-wood was eleven years ago, when Dad first planted the tree with us as feuding twin toddlers.

"Cormac didn't mean to *get* at you – he was just trying to do some funny stuff, using his own experiences."

Duh. I *knew* that. I saw a documentary on TV one night about the One Hundred Best

193

Comedians ever, and they all went on about observational humour, and how comedians had to use the things and people around them to get gags. So mostly today, *I'd* been the gag.

"You mean *my* experiences," I corrected Sonny, my eyes still firmly shut.

"Are you really annoyed, Sadie?" I heard Sonny ask, above the hum of buzzing bees and other humming somethings.

"At him for telling stories about me, or for you and Dad telling him stuff about me in the first place? Well, the answer's both!"

And I was pretty annoyed at myself for being horrible to Cormac in the first place, though I wasn't about to admit *that* to Sonny. If I hadn't goaded Cormac, he wouldn't have had any reason to stand up on his silly upturned box and talk about me.

"Yeah, well, he got at *me* too, y'know."

I didn't say anything. Why should I?

Tick, tock, tick, tock went the passing seconds. If Sonny wanted to bring up the boy band thing, it was up to him. I quite liked the idea of him squirming about it.

"And I *didn't* nick Dad's old room from you, by the way," Sonny carried on with his now diversifying conversation, even if I wasn't joining in. "Mum suggested it. I hadn't even *thought* of it."

Well, I guess that *last* bit made sense, what with him being an airhead and everything.

An airhead who was secretly in a *boy* band.

"And you know I just wanted to say . . . sort of . . . sorry."

What for? For being alive? For being my twin? For pirouetting unexpectedly at unusual times causing maximum mortification?

For secretly being in a *boy* band?

"Benny at school – the new tutor who started a couple of weeks ago? He wanted me and Kennedy and some of the other guys to audition for this kind of 'junior' boy band thing he'd come up with. I really didn't *want* to do it. I mean, you *know* I hate boy bands. But he's got a major label involved already, and it's just amazing exposure! And then . . . well, then I just *freaked*, thinking what you and Dad would make of it. . ."

I flipped back in my memory index, remembering Sonny being un-Sonny-ish and monosyllabic, grumpily volleying Dog over the wall with his football, walking out on me and Dad when we were mimicking boy band routines to "Chicken Payback", getting nabbed watching old boy band videos on the Hits channel, kicking the door shut when I caught him doing cheesy dance routines, getting ratty when Kennedy nearly blew his/their cover.

"The cycling shorts. . .!" I giggled, breaking my silence and opening my eyes. "That's not part of your 'costume', is it?"

"Yeah," sighed Sonny, daring to sit down beside me now that I seemed less likely to throw a rock at his head. "Rubbish, isn't it?"

"Totally!" I laughed, pushing myself up on to my elbows.

Actually, now that Sonny's dreaded secret was out in the open, I might as well have a laugh about it.

"So come on . . . what are you going to be called? Let me guess: Boys'r'Cool. Huh? Or how about Boyz Rock. Yeah? Or Boyz'n'Lycra!!"

Ah-ha! Sonny dropped his chin on to his chest. Had I nearly nailed it? Had I got close to the inevitably corny boy-band name?

"It's nothing like that," said Sonny, directly to his navel.

"So what *is* it like?" I asked, propping myself up further.

"Well, me and the other guys in the band, we were all suggesting stuff. And my suggestion sort of won," said Sonny, sort of apologetically, absolutely not looking me in the eye.

Ping!

A thought from his head, a ping of certainty, fired straight into mine.

"What?" I demanded, knowing a thousand per cent that it was something to do with *me*. "What is it?"

Sonny mumbled something I couldn't quite hear.

"I thought they taught you how to project your voice at stage school," I snapped at him. "Speak up!!"

"Um, we're called. . ." Sonny coughed a bit. "We're called 'Sadie Rocks. . .'"

"*Huh?*" I heard myself squeak, at the same time as I felt myself flush a warm puce.

"It's just . . . well, when we were all just chatting about stuff, I told them a bunch of stories about what a *grouch* you were, and one of the lads said, 'sounds like Sadie rocks!'. But y'know . . . meaning it *sarcastically* and everything. . ."

Sonny's voice dribbed away to a mumble, as if he had a mouth full of humble pie.

In the meantime, my mind whirled with the potential enormous embarrassment of it all.

I mean, hadn't he just said that there was a record company interested in the band already?

What if Sonny and his mates got famous? What if everyone in interviews asked them how they got their name, and all that stuff about me being a grouch came out?

Maybe I should build a hermit's hut out here by the Christmas tree and never come out, I decided. *Or at least not till everyone I know has died so I won't have to stand the shame.*

"Hey . . . Sadie?"

It was a wary voice. It came from over by a clump of nearby gravestones. I bent my head down a little to see through the greenery. First glance told me it wasn't a ghost.

"What?!" I called out to Cormac, who was hovering among the mossy stones and old flowers. In his black suit and tie, he couldn't have looked more at home than if he was draped in a white sheet.

"You left the park. . ." he said, looking fidgety and awkward.

"Do you blame me?" I replied, raising my eyebrows at him.

"Well, no – but you missed the bit where everyone clapped and cheered, and I said I owed it all to you. . ."

He looked sheepish. He looked like he wanted me to say it was OK.

I thought back to his routine today, and felt instantaneously confused. I mean, so, Sonny ("*Donny*") got a mention back in the park, but mostly it had been about *me*. *Zadie*. Which was kind of deeply uncomfortable, and at the same time . . . well, pretty much a novelty.

It made a change to be in the spotlight – me, the "dependable", "capable", *ordinary* half of the Bird twins. Specially when all my life so far it had felt like that spotlight was glimmering on my hyper-happy, annoying brother.

And speaking of the spotlight, my hyper-happy annoying brother was going to be in a band – with a record deal?! – that had my name in it. Was that so bad? Was it maybe . . . all right?

So I was the grouch, but this grouch was beginning to feel in a tiny way chuffed.

"Do you, uh, forgive me?" Cormac asked, his shoulders slumping in consternation.

"Guess I'll live," I shrugged back casually at Cormac.

I grabbed a pine cone from the ground and headed back to the house. Maybe I wasn't naturally good at happiness and all that stuff, but I suddenly felt *buzzy*.

After all, if I *wanted*, there was a new, bigger room to move into, with a great view of the

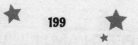

cemetery and everything. Plus there was the bubbling excitement of my own twin brother being in a band.

A *boy* band.

Oh, the hours, weeks, months and possibly *years* of teasing I was going to get out of this.

It was enough to make a grouch like me grin from ear to ear. . .

Make friends with Karen McCombie!

⋆ **Describe yourself in five words. . .**

Scottish, confident, shy, calm, ditzy.

⋆ **How did you become an author-girl?**

When I was eight, my teacher Miss Thomson told me I should write a book one day. I forgot about that for (lots of) years, then when I was working on teen mags, I scribbled a few short stories for them and suddenly thought, "Hmmm, I'd love to try and write a book . . . can I?"

⋆ **Where do you write your books?**

In the loft room at the top of our house. I work v. hard 'cause I only have a little bit of book-writing time – the rest of the day I'm making Playdough dinosaurs or pretend "cafés" with my little daughter, Milly.

⋆ **What else do you get up to when you're not writing?**

Reading, watching DVDs, eating crisps, patting cats and belly dancing!

Want to know more. . .?

Join Karen's club NOW!

For behind-the-scenes gossip on Karen's very own blog, fab competitions and funny photo galleries, become a fan member now on:

www.karenmccombie.com

P.S. Don't forget to send your bestest mate a groovy e-card once you've joined!

Karen says:

"It's sheeny and shiny, furry and er, funny in places! It's everything you could want from a website and a weeny bit more. . ."

What makes Sadie rock next? Book 2 is out now and totally brilliant!